DUSTY AYRES AND HIS BATTLE BIRDS:
THE RED DESTROYER

THE RED DESTROYER

By Robert Sidney Bowen

ALTUS PRESS • 2017

CHAPTER 1
VANISHING CRUISERS

EASING BACK the throttle, Dusty let the Silver Flash coast down to an easy landing on the High Speed Group 7 drome, just outside Springfield, Massachusetts. Taxiing swiftly up to the line he legged out and motioned a mechanic over to him. The man came on the run.

"Yes, skipper?"

"The left aileron wire's a bit slack," Dusty told him. "I guess you'd better touch it up a turn or two. Outside of that she seems O.K."

"As good as done now, sir," grinned the greaseball and went loping away for his tools.

Peeling off his flying jacket Dusty tossed it into the cockpit and headed toward the mess lounge. But before he reached it a field orderly trotted up to him.

"Major Drake's compliments, captain. You're wanted in the Group office."

"Right," nodded Dusty. Then asked, "Anything that can wait, corporal?"

The non-com shrugged.

"Don't know, sir," he said. "But Radio Officer Collins is with him. He seemed excited about something. And—"

Dusty didn't wait to hear the rest. He spun around, raced down the length of the mess building and shouldered in through

1

the group office door. Seated behind the desk was Major Drake, C.O. of the Group. On his right was the thin, flushed-faced figure of Collins. Dusty skidded to a halt and gave them both a sharp look.

DUSTY AYRES

"Anything wrong, sir?" he directed his question at the C.O.

Major Drake didn't answer. He scaled a radio form across the desk top. Dusty caught it and glanced at the typed message.

Captain Ayres

H.S.G No. 7

Stand by for action, three o'clock, at map position M 24.

Dusty read it twice, and looked up with a puzzled frown. "And from whom?" he demanded bluntly.

Major Drake shrugged.

"Your guess is as good as ours," he said. "Collins got it out of the air ten minutes ago. Decided to wait 'til you landed, instead of calling you down. Did you note that map position reading?"

Dusty glanced at it again, and suddenly stiffened.

"What the—" he gulped. "Unless I'm crazy, M Twenty-four is about five or six hundred miles due east of the Massachusetts coast."

"You're not crazy," grunted the C.O. "That's just where it is. And to add more fog to the picture, read this. It's a decoded Navy order that was sent out this morning. In ease you don't know, each of these letters is a battle cruiser."

Dusty took the second message form the C.O. held out.

Emergency H-K-L. Position XXX-2. Proceed at once to M 24 for skirmish attack on small enemy force reported in surrounding waters.

U.S.N. 12

"Well, at least this reads authentic," said Dusty, as he dropped the form on the desk. "Twelve is Admiral Standers, chief of Naval Staff, isn't he?"

"Right again," nodded the C.O. "Now tell me why the Chief of Naval Staff would personally send out a coded order to three ships to skirmish-attack a small enemy force?"

"He wouldn't!" answered Dusty promptly. "Or it would at least be relayed through the Battle Force commander. Say, how about checking with Naval H.Q.?"

The C.O. jerked a thumb toward the teletype set on the corner of his desk.

"Waiting for a check-back on my question, now," he said. "It should be along at any—"

At that moment the machine started clicking and cut off the rest of the sentence. As one man the three of them leaned forward and fastened their eyes on the moving strip of ticker tape. One by one the letters appeared upon it.

CO.-H.S.G. 7 —NO-SUCH-ORDER-SENT-OUT —
CHECK-BACK-WITH COMPLETE-DETAILS—12.

As the machine went silent Dusty glanced at his watch. The hands showed exactly five minutes of two. Reaching out, he tapped the unsigned radio message.

"That's not an order, sir," he said grimly. "That's an invitation. And I'd better be going or I'll be late."

"Hey, what the devil do you mean?" Drake stopped him as he turned toward the door. "And where are you going?"

"To M Twenty-four," Dusty answered, jerking open the door. "I've been wondering if that rat was alive, ever since I came to in the hospital after the Chihuahua show."

"The Hawk?" shouted the C.O. struggling to his feet. "Don't be crazy! You must have killed him when you winged him as he left that Strato ship. He hasn't been seen or heard of since. And that's official from Washington Intelligence H.Q. Besides, you're in no condition for active flying. You take it easy while I check some more with Standers."

Dusty grinned and shook his head.

"Sorry, sir," he said. "But the old hunch is working again. The Hawk has sent me another invite—and I've never turned down one yet."

The C.O. started to object again, but Dusty ducked out tire door and ran over to his plane.

"Snap it up, Jones!" he called to the mechanic working on the aileron wire. "I'll give you just one minute to finish that."

"A minute you save, skipper," grinned the other, stuffing a turn-buckle wrench into his pocket. "She's oke, now."

DUSTY NODDED his thanks and had started to leg into the cockpit when a hand touched his shoulder.

"Tell papa about it! You're in too much of a rush for a little boy only two days out of the hospital."

Dusty turned to stare into "Curly" Brooks' grinning face. He grimaced, shrugged off the detaining hand and got into his cockpit.

"Nothing, sweetheart, nothing," he said, snapping up the switch. "I've simply been invited to a party."

"I like parties."

"Sure! And nix! You'd get under the feet of us grown-ups."

With that, Dusty kicked the electric starter, caught the engine on the first rev and sent the Silver Flash streaking across the field.

Pulling the plane clear he poked the nose up in a steep climbing turn. And when he presently reached twenty-five thousand he leveled off and set the robot pilot on a due east course. Leaning back against the head-rest he stared thoughtfully at the instrument board.

"Too crude for even the Blacks to try,'" he murmured aloud. "Yet, that was from that bum, or I'm a Chinaman! Oh well, old girl, we're at least going places, and that's something isn't it?"

As he spoke he reached out his free hand and slapped the side of the cockpit. After two weeks of being flat on his back in a base hospital, with medicos and orderlies fussing over him, it was like a new lease on life to be back in the game again. Yeah, it sure was—

He cut off the rest of the joyful thought as the red signal light on the radio panel suddenly started blinking. Snapping on reception volume he spun the wave-length dial. As it reached the S.O.S.-Emergency reading strange sounds crackled in the ear-phones.

He listened in frowning puzzlement a few seconds before he realized that he was on the U.S. Navy official S.O.S. length, and that some operator was transmitting a coded message to Washington H.Q.

Not knowing the code, it all meant nothing to him, and he was about to switch off when his eye fell on the station directional-finder dial. The message was being sent from a sea station located between five hundred and a thousand miles due east of his own position.

"From M Twenty-Four, by God!" he gasped.

At that instant, as though confirming his own statement, the code message stopped abruptly and English words crackled out of the ear-phones.

"Emergency relief to M Twenty-four! Hurry! Cruisers *Texas*, *Utah* and *Vermont* sunk without trace. Enemy air force now approaching from north. Pilot Vance of the *Texas* calling for help from the air. Our ships were destroyed by...."

The earphones emitted a noise that sounded like a yelp of pain and then went silent. The blood surging wildly through his veins, Dusty turned on full volume and fiddled frantically with the wave-length dial. But it was a waste of time. The earphones remained silent.

As a last resort he turned the set on transmission and called back Pilot Vance on his own emergency wave-length. But that also was a waste of time. Other stations were trying to do the same thing, and the result was static jamming on all wave-lengths. The high-keyed hum in his phones told Dusty that much.

Snapping off the set altogether he checked with his roller map and compass, veered a bit toward the northeast, and sent the Silver Flash thundering out over the Atlantic at maximum revs.

Hunching forward over the stick he glued his eyes on the distant horizon, and sat like a man of stone. Seconds whipped past and became minutes. More seconds and more minutes. And then suddenly he sucked in his breath sharply, and automatically jerked up both thumbs against the electric trigger trips of his twin Brownings cowled into the nose forward.

FAR AHEAD, and just a shade to his left, a swarm of dots were faintly silhouetted against a sun-glistening cloud bank. To tell their make or type was impossible at the distance. Yet, as he peered at them a strange and eerie feeling rippled up and down his spine. In days and months gone by that same feeling

"TAKE IT, SAP!", SHOUTED DUSTY, AND SENT A WITHERING BURST LASHING DOWN AT THE GLASS COWLING

had often come to him—and it had always resulted in ultimate gunfire action.

"And that will be O.K. with me!" he grunted grimly. "We need practice, old girl. So get going! At—"

He didn't end the sentence. A brilliant shaft of sun-light had caught the dot nearest to him. Instantly it changed in shape; ceased to be a dot any longer, and took on the dim outline of a pontooned biplane.

One glance at it and Dusty knew beyond all doubt that it was a U.S. Navy plane. It was cutting sharp west and racing toward shore. And tearing after it were five jet-black monoplanes.

The sight of the Black ships drove all doubts from Dusty's mind. The Blacks had cut in to attack Vance of the *Texas* before he had a chance to complete his message. Undoubtedly a burst had nailed his radio and put it out for good. And now the navy pilot, possibly wounded, was racing nose down for American waters with a pack of vultures at his heels.

All speculation, of course, but Dusty didn't waste time seeking proof of his thoughts. Time for that, later. Right now a Yank pilot was in a tough spot.

Slapping the Flash around on wing-tip he sent it slicing down toward the lead Black ship. At the same instant he jabbed both trigger trips forward and spat hot steel across the sky.

Even for his Brownings the range was too great. But that didn't matter at the moment. If he could only attract the atten-tion of the Blacks long enough for the Yank navy man to increase his lead, that would be plenty.

As the end of the next five seconds proved, he did more than that. He not only attracted their attention, he lured them toward his position.

Perhaps it was recognition of the Silver Flash, or perhaps it wasn't. But, at any rate, the Black Darts wheeled about in group attack formation and came charging at him.

"Greetings, you bums!" he roared aloud. "Where's the rest of you?"

As he spoke the last he pulled the Silver Flash up on its tail and climbed straight heavenward.

By leaning over and looking down through the glass cowl he could see the Blacks trying to claw up toward him. He grinned tightly, held the Flash nose-up for a few seconds longer, then started to haul it over on its back, as though he were completing the first half of a gigantic loop. But even as he started the maneuver he checked it and went slicing over in a lightning-like half roll.

A thousand other pilots might have tried it and failed. But Dusty's timing was perfect. Like a roaring bullet he came out directly above the lead Black plane.

Its pilot had leveled off, intending to nail him as he slid down the back of the loop. But now it was too late. Dusty had him cold. Even as the Yank jabbed his trigger trips he saw the cruel featured but startled face that turned up to gape at him.

"Take it!" shouted Dusty and sent a withering burst lashing down at the glass cowling.

For perhaps a full second the Dart hung motionless in the air. And then, as though a giant sledgehammer had smashed down upon it, the nose dropped and the plane went thundering downward with a dead pilot still grasping its control stick.

Dusty didn't waft to watch it slice into the waters of the Atlantic far below. He was too busy with enemy number two. And he got it in as many minutes.

Made-in-the-U.S.A. steel ripped and tore into Dart wing stubs and beat a savage tattoo against the engine cowling. The Black pilot tried frantically to full roll out and then spin down into the clear. But his frantic efforts spelled his doom. The bullet-weakened wing stubs refused to stand the added strain, and as though it were actually made of so much paper, the right wing tore off and went slip-sliding away. The rest pivoted about crazily for an instant and then dropped like a rock straight down into oblivion.

But though Dusty's trick attack got results, there were still four Darts left in the air. And the losing of two of their comrades must have fired them, with berserk and wreckless rage. For, without bothering to form close attack formation, they went darting in at Dusty like brain-flamed vultures.

"Tough, eh?" taunted the Yank as he went skidding into the clear in the nick of time. "My, my, am I all surprised!"

Kicking back in a snap reverse he pounced on the nearest Black and started to draw a bead on the glass cowling. But he never hit it. At that moment all hell came swooping down from above. One of the other three Blacks had looped, and now his bullets were smacking into the Silver Flash.

With a howl of rage at having been caught at his own game, Dusty flung the Flash up on wing-tip and cut downward like a bolt of lightning. However, the Blacks were playing their own game now, and a split second later invisible fingers poked holes through Dusty's cowling. Stinging glass splinters whipped back to cut into his cheeks. And for one hellish second his brain went ice cold as he waited for the sensation of a sizzling hot spear of steel slicing through his heart. But, whether due to luck or instinctive flying skill, the hot spear of steel didn't hit him and he went tearing out from under the blistering burst.

Faking a sharp left turn he hauled back on the stick with all his might and sent the Silver Flash sky-rocketing upward. But almost in the same instant he wheeled over and darted off to one side. The looping Black had gone up again, and was waiting for him.

"Like hell you will!" grated Dusty savagely. "I don't hanker to be a dumb cluck twice in the same day!"

In what was practically one continuous movement of the controls he slammed the Flash up and over on its back and went corkscrewing diagonally downward. The top Black tried to follow him through but his plane half stalled and fell off on one wing.

Cutting back in a wing-groaning reverse Dusty caught him cold in a perfect broadside attack. The Black probably never knew what hit him.

Dusty's long burst plowed through the engine cowling and chewed a fuel line to shreds. Raw fuel spilling out on a hot over-revving engine did the rest. There was a sheet of livid flame, a terrific roar, and the Dart was a shower of pieces slithering down.

THE INSTANT the sheet of flame leaped out, Dusty cut his fire, pulled the Flash up in a screaming zoom and glanced downward for a glimpse of the two remaining Blacks. As he did, his eyes widened and a sharp exclamation of dumbfounded surprise spilled off his lips.

One of the two Blacks was spinning seaward in flames, and the other was twisting and turning all over the sky as its pilot strived desperately to get clear of the withering fire that poured out from the guns of an all blue American plane.

"Curly!" Dusty bellowed aloud. "Well, I'll be damned!"

Ramming the nose of the Flash straight down to the vertical, he pounced upon the Black ship as it came whipping out of a two-turn spin.

His Brownings yammered out one short burst, and that was that. The Black didn't have the chance to even glance upward. Steel death smashed down through his glass cockpit cowl and buried itself in his skull.

Like a kite whose ground cord has snapped in two the Dart went skidding around crazily, and finally went plunging nose-on for the rolling waters of the Atlantic.

Without giving it a second glance Dusty pulled but of his dive, eased back the throttle and swung in close to Curly's ship. Across the air space his lanky pal gave him a trick salute and grinned from ear to ear. Dusty returned it with a gesture of poking someone in the jaw, and then spun his wave-length dial to Curly's reading.

"Where the hell did you come from?" he demanded.

Chuckling sound came out of the ear phones.

"Me? Oh, I was just passing by, and I thought I'd drop in."

"Yeah?" Dusty cracked back. "Well, I've got something for you, sweetheart, when we land. But thanks just the same, guy. Maybe those last two would have slipped away. But seriously, Curly, how come you knew I was here?"

"Got the news from a little bird named Drake," the ear-phones replied. "And, well you know—papa likes to keep an eye on you. But say, did you hear that S.O.S. call from that navy man? What—"

"Save it, Curly!" cut in Dusty. "Other ears, you know. Tag me and we'll chin later."

Snapping off the contact Dusty banked around and headed for shore. Though there was no way of telling definitely, he guessed that the Navy plane had headed for the air base just north of Portsmouth, N.H.—and he wanted to have a talk with Pilot Vance.

For one thing he wanted to find out how the three battle cruisers had been destroyed. It was a cinch that the Black Darts hadn't done the job. The type of bombs they carried would have been no more effective than cream puffs against the armored decks of the cruisers.

"And another thing," grunted Dusty, continuing his train of thought aloud, "they were some of the Hawk's brood. What the hell were they doing way out at M Twenty-Four?"

That none of them had been the Hawk, himself, he knew quite definitely. Too many times had he tangled props with the air ace of the Black Invaders not to instantly recognize the man's style of combat flying. No, the Hawk hadn't been with that bunch.

"But he was back of it!" he grated harshly. "I know damn well he was!"

Fully convinced of that one fact he urged the Flash on to maximum speed in an effort to contact Pilot Vance as soon as possible. Presently the tip of Cape Ann, Massachusetts, slid up over the eastern horizon, and he started to veer a degree or two to the northwest when, suddenly, the radio signal light blinked rapidly.

A glance told him that a message was coming in on his own emergency wave-length. Reaching out he spun the dial and grabbed up the transmitter tube.

"Captain Ayres contacting!" he called. "Go ahead!"

"Washington H.Q. calling you, captain," the ear-phones barked. "Orders from X Thirty-Four. Report at once! This is an emergency order. Check back, please!"

Dusty bit his lip and scowled at the radio panel. X-34 was the official designation of General Horner, chief of U.S. Intelligence and father of Agent 10. That he was sending out an emergency order meant something important was in the wind. Yet, hell, Pilot Vance was probably at Portsmouth Base, and he wanted—

He cut off the thought and beat over the transmitter tube.

"Reporting shortly, Washington!" he said. "Please cut contact; I've another call to make!"

The instant the click in the phones indicated that Washington had gone off the air, he spun the wave-length dial to the Portsmouth Base reading.

"Captain Ayres calling Portsmouth Base!"

Two seconds later he received the check-back.

"Portsmouth Base on your wave! Go ahead!"

"Did Pilot Vance of the U.S.S. *Texas* land at—"

Dusty cut off the rest with a gasp, jerked up straight in the seat, and stared hard at a strip of barren and rocky shoreline just off his left wings. Crumpled up against a large jagged point of rock was a pontooned plane with U.S. Navy Air Force insignia on each side of its fuselage. And on the tail fin encircled by a heavy blue line was a large red T.

"Vance!" gulped Dusty unconsciously nosing down. "And he cracked up!"

Totally oblivious to the frantic calls from Portsmouth Base crackling in his ear-phones, he went thundering down, leveled off about fifty feet over the water and went streaking past the wrecked ship. And it was then that he saw the huddled figure hanging half out of the crushed cockpit. One hand raised slowly up, fluttered weakly at him and then dropped back and hung swinging like a broken cable.

Decision and action became one to Dusty. Belting his ship around in a flash half turn he went racing in toward shore.

CHAPTER 2
YELLOW LIGHTNING

A HUNDRED yards in from the rocks he found a small square of cleared ground. It was furrowed and ridged, and a perfect crack-up graveyard for a fledgling pilot. But it was just another field to Dusty, and cutting his throttle and prop he slid down into it and made an easy brake-wind landing.

Leaping out he pounded back toward the waters edge, peeling off his flying jacket and tunic as he ran. When he reached it he paused long enough to kick off his field boots and then plunged into icy cold water. The instant he hit it his feet and arms were working like greased pistons.

The crumpled ship lay about fifty yards off shore, but he reached the jagged point against which it was jammed in less time than it takes to tell. But that was when his real troubles began. The sides of the spear-shaped rock were caked with slime.

A dozen times he tried to get a hold and pull himself up, but each time his clawing fingers slipped and he flopped back into the water.

The plane had crashed pontoon first and then slumped over to the right. From his position in the water he could not see Pilot Vance, but he could hear the man groaning faintly.

"Chin up, Vance!" he panted, swimming around to the seaward side of the rock. "Chin up, old man!"

"Hurry—hurry! Want to tell you—"

The husked words trailed off to a gurgling groan.

Abandoning all further attempt to climb up the rock itself, Dusty flung a hand upward and grabbed hold of the ripped step of the pontoon.

Sharp dural edges cut into his fingers, but he gritted his teeth against the pain and hauled himself up so that he could hook his other arm around one of the broken pontoon struts. From that position he was able to wiggle up onto the lower right wing.

Pausing but an instant to catch his breath he worked his way along to the crushed fuselage and the huddled figure in the cockpit. Bracing himself as best he could he reached out and lifted the still figure up to a slumping sitting position. A blood smeared face greeted his gaze.

"Vance! Vance! Can you talk, old man?

Eyelids fluttered open, and bloodshot orbs stared at him dully. A second later the pain whitened lips quivered and whispered words drifted out from between them.

"Thanks, Ayres—didn't mean—to run—away. Rats—got me! Was trying to—to reach—to reach—Portsmouth. Guess—passed out—and crashed. I—"

THE REST was blotted out as the man coughed violently, and blood flecked the corners of his mouth. Dusty groaned helplessly and waited for the coughing spasm to pass. When it did, he leaned close to the man.

"Hang on, Vance! Don't try to talk. Just try to hang on while I go for help!"

The other's head moved slowly from side to side, and he raised one hand in feeble protest.

"Can't do—anything!" he mumbled. "Got—lungs. Must tell you—before it's too—late."

Once more the blood spattering coughing spell choked off the man's words. His chest seemed to cave inward, and his eyes fluttered closed. For an instant Dusty thought that he had gone for good.

"Come back, Vance!" he yelled. "What happened—tell me what happened?"

The navyman's eyes remained closed, but his blue-white lips moved.

"Don't know—exactly. Steaming north—on orders for skirmish attack—and—"

"But that order was never sent out!" Dusty interrupted before he could check himself.

The bloodshot eyes opened for an instant.

"Course it was! Saw Sparks—give it to—the Old Man! We steamed—north—*Texas* in lead. Sent aloft for—advance scouting. Didn't see a thing. Then—then, suddenly, I—"

"Yes, yes?" cried Dusty, as the navy-man faltered and stopped. "What happened?"

"The—the bow of the *Texas* was sticking—out of water! The boilers went up—and she was gone. At the same instant my ship went into—a spin. Lost five hundred feet in a gale. Damn near ripped—my wings off!"

As the man paused again, Dusty said nothing. He simply stared down at the blood smeared face, a tiny frown creasing his forehead. A moment later he impulsively reached out and touched Vance on the shoulder.

"A gale, Vance?" he asked. "It couldn't have been a gale, old man. The sky was practically cloudless when I got there."

"Must have been a gale," the pain-twisted lips whispered. "Lightning—too. A great sheet of yellow lightning. Almost—struck me. Only missed me—by inches. Next thing I knew—*Utah* was—only ship on the—water. Then—it broke in two—amidships—and sank. Yellow lightning—Darts attacked—got me—tried to call Washington—call Washington—call-call—"

"Wait, Vance, wait! You've got to live, old man! You can't go—!"

Dusty finished the rest with a groan. It was useless to yell at the navyman, now. The tiny thread that separates human life from death had parted, and whatever else Vance might have said was sealed in the brain of a dead man.

For a long moment Dusty stood motionless, trying to make even a little bit of sense out of what he had just heard But presently a hail from shore jerked him out of his befuddled reverie.

"Hey! Need me out there?"

Dusty turned to see Curly standing on the lip of the shore ledge. He shook his head, and cupped a hand to his lips.

"No use now, Curly!" he yelled. "I'm coming ashore. You call Portsmouth Base. Tell them Pilot Vance is here—dead!"

As he saw Brooks turn away from the shore he crawled out on the wing and let his body drop off into the water. Five minutes later he was back on shore and squeezing what water he could out of his sea logged clothes. And by the time Curly came running back from the planes he had jammed his feet into his field boots and was pulling on his tunic.

"Vance, eh?" was Brooks' first question.

Dusty simply nodded. Curly glared at him.

"Secrets?" he snapped. "Or am I allowed to know?"

Dusty finished buttoning up his tunic and held out his hand.

"Give me a cigarette, and I'll tell you."

After Curly had complied and had lighted up he told his pal the whole story in detail. Brooks listened right to the end in frowning silence.

"Poor devil, probably didn't even realize that he was talking!" Curly grunted as Dusty finished. "Much less what he was talking about. I'm wondering if he really did see three cruisers go down."

Dusty toed out his cigarette, and shrugged.

"We can check up on that with the Navy Department," he said. "But something must have happened to one of them!"

"Huh? What do you mean?"

"The *Texas*," Dusty replied. "Vance was from the *Texas*, you know. And I didn't see a single cruiser in the M Twenty-Four area. Did you?"

Brooks' eyes widened.

"Gee, that's so. No, I didn't. But, listen, here's something. Where did those Darts come from? They were members of the Hawk's brood."

"I'm wondering that, too," Dusty nodded grimly. "They probably came from the Hawk's regular drome. But what I want to know, is—were they there on orders?"

"If the Hawk sent you that radio," said Curly slowly, "my

guess is, yes! What Vance got was planned for you. But, sending only five was a dumb stunt. But, here's something that maybe you don't know—the Hawk's drome was abandoned a week ago, while you were in hospital."

Dusty started, then relaxed.

"Probably picked out a new field," he said. "It's being done, you know."

"That's just the idea?" cut in Brooks quickly. "Assuming that that radio was from the Hawk; up until today none of us have heard of, or seen, the Black Hawk—or any of his brood!"

"You mean—?"

"Yeah! Not a single Black Dart has been sighted for a week. Not a one! I was almost beginning to think that they'd washed out the type."

DUSTY SCOWLED savagely at the sky as a thousand and one infinitesimal pieces of a cockeyed and crazy mystery puzzle floated and danced before his mind's eye.

"It must make sense, somehow!" he grunted, speaking more to himself than to Curly. "We just can't figure it out—yet."

"Check," nodded Brooks. "So what?"

"You got Portsmouth?" asked Dusty.

"I did. A relief boat must be on the way down now."

"Then there's no use hanging around here," said Dusty, starting toward the planes. "General Horner sent me an S.O.S. order to report to him. You'd better shove on back to the field, and I'll chase down to Washington."

Brooks cursed softly.

"You may be the fair-haired boy to H.Q. staff," he snorted,

"but you're a pain in the neck to me. I'm tagging with you—and no buts!"

Dusty started to speak, then changed his mind and grinned.

"O.K." he said. "I'd probably find you at Washington field when I landed, anyway. But listen, my big brave guardian, if anything happens, you follow my orders! Get it?"

Curly gestured humble acquiescence.

"I wouldn't even dream of doing otherwise!" he murmured.

Dusty shot him a final warning look and legged into the cockpit of the Flash. Half a minute later he had pulled the wheels clear and was clawing air for altitude. Because of his bullet-shattered glass cowl he leveled off at ten thousand, waited for Curly to swing in behind and then set a compass course down the coast line toward the nation's capital.

Slumping back against the headrest he reviewed once more the sequence of events that had taken place since Major Drake called him into the Group office.

The net result was simply additional confirmation of his already definite belief that the Black Hawk was alive, and was the keyman of a new mysterious war thrust at the United States. Beyond that, everything else was a mixed-up jumble of intangible items.

The one upon which he pondered the most was Pilot Vance's raving statement that the three U.S. battle cruisers had gone down in almost no time at all.

"Vance must have been out of his head!" he muttered aloud. "They didn't go at the same time. Were they all asleep? Hell,

someone was bound to see what hit them. Sure! And I would
have picked up their distress calls. Why—"

On impulse he left the rest hanging in midair, shot out his
free hand and spun the wave-length dial. "Captain Ayres calling
Navy H.Q., Washington!" he spoke into the transmitter tube.
"Captain Ayres calling Navy H.Q. on Seven-Two-Six!"

He repeated the call four times before the red signal light
on the panel blinked. A voice spoke in his phones, but it was
so muffled that he had to strain his ears to catch the words.

"Navy H.Q. on your wave! Proceed!"

"Can you give me a position report on the *Texas, Utah* and
Vermont?" he yelled.

TWO OR three minutes of silence followed, during which
time the phones emitted a sort of fuzzy sound. Dusty fingered
the dial to tune it out, but the noise continued. Face grim he
bent over the transmitter tube.

"Station tuning in on Seven-Two-Six, get off!" he snapped.
"You are garbling reception! Oh, Navy H.Q.! A check-back on
my question, please!"

The fuzzy sound continued in the phones, but presently
Dusty caught the voice of the Navy H.Q. operator.

"Position of ships unreported since six o'clock this morning.
Have you any information? Admiral's orders to report it at
once!"

Dusty opened his lips to speak, hesitated, and clamped them
shut. The familiar sensation was again rippling up and down
his spine. The continuance of the fuzzy noise caused it. Some
other station was tuning in directly on the Seven-Two-Six

wave-length. And it was a station that operated on a different frequency, and therefore could not get clear tuning-in. It was either that, or else there was some sort of static disturbance near the station.

Hesitating a moment longer he suddenly spoke into the transmitter tube.

"Ships sighted ten minutes ago, Navy!" he called. "They were steaming a course up the Maine coast. Just wondered if an air escort was needed."

The Navy H.Q. operator started to speak, but suddenly the fuzzy sound increased in tone and the voice was blotted out. Dusty cursed and tried to regain contact on a different wave-length, and failed. Finally he snapped off the set in disgust, and sat glowering at it.

A moment later, though, the signal light blinked rapidly on the S.O.S. dial reading. He snapped on and grabbed the transmitter tube.

"Navy H.Q.?" he called eagerly.

"No, captain. But perhaps I can answer your question."

Dusty's body went rigid, and an agate glint sprang into his eyes. Even in his sleep he would instantly recognize the owner of that voice.

"You, Hawk, eh?" he grated. "Where are you, rat? I thought we had a little date!"

The earphones chuckled harshly, and then came words.

"We did my friend, and I must apologize. I should have made it an hour earlier. Those battle cruisers steamed to M Twenty-Four sooner than I expected. And after I had destroyed them,

I could not wait for you. But, one of my flights entertained you, did it not?"

It was Dusty's turn to laugh.

"Not very much," he said. "There weren't enough of them. And by the way, don't expect them home for supper!"

"That is regrettable," purred the earphones. "However, the officers and crew of three of your finest battle cruisers will not be home to supper, either, as you term it. And they are only the beginning."

As the Black spoke Dusty regulated his directional finder needle, and found that the Hawk's position was due south of him. He opened the throttle wide, and bent over the transmitter tube again.

"Tell me," he said, stalling for time in which to race south. "I suppose you did it all by your little self? And if so, how-come I saw them not fifteen minutes ago?"

The phones chuckled again.

"Your Navy H.Q. may believe that, captain. But, I know that you lie. Your Navy H.Q. told the truth. Those three battle cruisers have been unreported since six o'clock this morning. Their wave-lengths have been static-jammed. Even that S.O.S. call of Pilot Vance did not get through to Washington. And their position right now is somewhere at the bottom of the Atlantic ocean!"

"Yeah?" echoed Dusty, as little fingers of icy truth curled about his heart. "Well, Pilot Vance got through to me! Your vultures didn't get him—and he told me the whole story."

"So?" grated the phones. "They did not kill him? Then they

deserved to die! They had their orders. But, your bluff is useless, captain. It was impossible for Pilot Vance to tell you anything. And would you care for proof of that fact?"

The fingers of Dusty's free hand curled into a steel hard fist.

"What I'd like," he gritted, "is another date with you! They tell me you've been too yellow to show your ugly mug, lately. Still yellow?"

"Words, captain, just words! There are times when I must put aside my personal desires. However, should you care for another meeting, I believe I have time to accommodate you. Shall we say, in an hour—above your city of Boston?"

"Perfect, perfect!" Dusty grinned into the transmitter tube. "I'll be there with bells on!"

"And so will I, captain," came the harshly chuckled words. "But—be sure to keep your eyes open!"

A wild, grating laugh blasted out of the phones, and then the set clicked silent.

CHAPTER 3
THE INVISIBLE ACE

FOR A long moment Dusty sat perfectly still. But inwardly he was quivering with wild excitement. It seemed years since he'd tangled with his old enemy. And now that another meeting was in the offing savage joy gripped him from head to foot.

Perhaps the meeting would result in a few answers to the hundred odd questions that spun around in his brain. Or, perhaps, it wouldn't. But, one way or the other, it didn't matter at the moment. The main item was that he would meet the Black Hawk.

The flash of wings out of the corner of his eye, brought back the realization that he was not alone. He stared out across the air-space as Curly swung in close; saw the happy grin on his pal's face. The grin told him that Curly had been listening in, and was as tickled as he.

Shaking his head vigorously he made waving-away motions with his free hand. Curly's grin faded, and he scowled stubbornly. Spinning the wave-length dial, Dusty got him on contact.

"Orders, kid," he said. "This is personal. Buzz off and buy yourself a stick of candy. I'll see you later."

"My pal!" the phones snarled. "But some day I'll be famous, too, you mug! Luck!"

To Dusty's surprise Curly banked off and went thundering westward. He followed the ship out of sight, a half sad smile on his lips.

"Don't make them any better!" he grunted aloud. "Wish he could come along at that."

Turning his eyes front he brushed all thought of Curly from his mind, and concentrated on getting ready for his meeting with the Hawk. His ammo belts still had plenty of slugs in them. In the scrap with the Darts he had made every shot tell, and he still had plenty left for the Hawk.

His only regret was that his glass cowling was in splinters. That meant that he had to keep low, with the result that the Hawk would have the advantage of getting peak altitude when-

He saw the Federal Building cave
in like a house built of sand.

ever it was necessary. The thought of that brought a tight grin to Dusty's lips.

"Let him!" he snapped. "I'll spot that rat ten thousand any day, and beat him to the punch. Only hope that he isn't too yellow to come down to my front yard!"

With a final check of the instruments and guns he veered a bit inshore and stared hard at the horizon ahead. Low down on it he could see the towering buildings of Boston poking their blunt and pointed tops skyward. And beyond it the harbor in which both merchant and war ships rode lazily at anchor. Save for those warships there was not a single hint of war about the thriving metropolis.

But Dusty only gave the city a glance. The air above it took all of his attention. Hunched forward over the stick he literally scrutinized every cubic inch-—and saw nothing to make the blood dance through his veins. His watch told him that he was five minutes early.

Easing back the throttle a bit he coasted lazily about over the Hub's suburbs, always keeping an alert eye aloft. Minutes dragged by and eventually his watch told him that the Hawk was half an hour late.

A tremor of marked disappointment rippled through him, and he was on the point of speeding down to Washington to answer General Horner's summons, when suddenly the red signal light blinked. He snapped on contact, and spoke into the transmitter tube.

"Go ahead!"

"You are waiting, captain?" came the voice of the Hawk in

the ear-phones. "Sorry to be late again. Watch closely my friend—watch very closely!"

AS THE set clicked off, Dusty screwed around in the seat and stared hard up at the sky. But not a single plane did he see. Not even a tiny dot that might be the Hawk thundering down upon him. He poked the nose of the Flash upward, at full gun, to get a better view.

But it availed him nothing. Save for himself, he was absolutely alone in the air. He grated out a curse, and rapped his clenched fist against the side of the cockpit.

"Bluff again!" he growled. "The rat's too yellow to take a chance. The hell with him, then!"

He slapped the Flash around and started south across the city. But a split second later he went rigid in the seat, and a wild cry of alarm burst from his lips. About a mile ahead of him, on the harbor front of Boston, stood the towering Federal Building—a massive pillar of steel and stone that rose up for an even one hundred stories.

And now, as he gaped at it, hardly daring to believe his eyes, he saw it cave in in the center, and crumble apart like a house of sun-baked sand. Its two spires snapped off like match sticks and went hurtling down into the streets below.

The four walls visibly rocked back and forth and then collapsed inward, as though their very foundations had been smashed out from under them. Smoke and fire belched upward, the licking tongues of red seeming to almost singe the fleecy clouds high overhead. And the roar of a terrific explosion rent the sky.

In a matter of split seconds the city became a seething inferno of utter chaos. Like a man struck dumb, Dusty sat gaping down at the horrible sight. Panic reigned for a full mile around the crumpled building.

The streets were choked with fear-gripped men, women and children fighting to get away from the stricken area. And like ants quitting their hills, thousands more poured out of the other buildings to add to the berserk chaos in the streets.

"An earthquake! My God, it's an earthquake!"

Above the roar of his own engine, Dusty suddenly became conscious of the sound of his own voice. It jerked him back to partial sanity, and he snapped out his hand and spun the wave-length dial to Washington H.Q.

"Washington, Washington!" he bellowed into the transmitter tube. "Earthquake at Boston! Federal Building completely destroyed. Order help to this area at once. Emergency! Captain Ayres calling you. I'm over the city now!"

As he paused for breath, General Horner's voice suddenly boomed out of the earphones.

"What's that, Ayres? The Federal Building destroyed? Oh my God! That wasn't—"

The rest was drowned out by a high keyed hum in the phones. Dusty recognized the noise in the flash of an instant. His contact with Washington was being static-jammed. He cursed, snapped off the set, took a final look at the horrible sight below, and sent the Flash roaring dead-on for Washington.

There was nothing that he could do at Boston. And his meeting with the Hawk was a disappointment of the past, now.

Washington H.Q. was his objective. Twice he had been static-jammed out of contact. Something was up. What? He didn't know. Couldn't even guess. He just felt it, inside.

Feeding the Flash's powerplant all it could take he raced down across Connecticut and New York. As he roared over eastern Pennsylvania the red signal light blinked. The instant he snapped on contact, the grating voice of the Hawk blasted against his ear-drums.

"Did you watch closely, captain? But then, of course you did. I heard you calling Washington. It was not an earthquake, my friend—but something far more effective. And a pretty sight, wasn't it?"

"Go sell your apples!" Dusty roared at him. "I knew you were too yellow to show your mug. And I'm busy, now!"

"But I did show myself, captain," the other purred back. "That you did not see me, is your fault. Yet, I do not blame you for having missed me. But—watch closely, I'll show myself again."

Dusty laughed harshly and cut off the set.

"Yeah!" he grated. "Maybe you'll send me a picture!"

Brushing all thought of the Hawk from his mind, he slanted the Flash downward a bit to get greater speed. Presently the Capitol eased up over the distant horizon. He swung a bit west, toward the military field and leveled off.

And then without warning, it happened.

One instant he was flying a dead-on course, and the next he was whipping wing over wing, like a sheet of paper in a gale of wind. Before he could check himself he was flung forward against the instrument board. His forehead smashed into the bowl compass and a thousand colored stars danced before his eyes.

Half groggy, he managed somehow to pull out of his crazy maneuver and right the plane. Through blurred eyes he searched the heavens and saw nothing but sun bathed air. There wasn't any more than a fistful of clouds in the sky. Brain doing loops, he slumped back against the head rest and rubbed his free hand across his eyes.

"Must be nuts!" he mumbled. "Or maybe I'm dreaming. But what the hell happened?"

As though to answer his question, it happened again!

A GIANT invisible hand grabbed his plane and flung it up and outward in a great curving arc. This time he had instinctively braced himself, but though he battled with the controls the Flash continued to cartwheel across the heavens. Finally, though, he smacked it up on even keel, steeled his jangling nerves as best he could and looked about. The picture was still the same—sun, air, a bit of clouds, and nothing else.

Suddenly, he realized that the red signal light was blinking. Automatically, he snapped on the set and spun the wave-length dial.

"You understand, now, captain?" came the taunting words. "Did you see me that time?"

"My God, where in hell are you?" Dusty blurted out without thinking.

"In the air, my friend," came the reply. "And in a position to kill you at will. But no, captain, do not be afraid. I shall not kill

"OUT, CURLY!
BAIL OUT--BAIL OUT!"

you—yet. After the annoyance you have caused me in the past, I insist that you live to witness my complete triumph."

The voice paused for a moment. Dusty started to speak but cut it off short as the earphones crackled again.

"But your friend is unimportant, captain. He approaches from the west, now. Watch, and you will see what I can do to you, any time I wish."

Even as the man spoke Dusty had slammed around and was racing westward. About five miles away, and a few thousand feet above him, a plane was bearing down on the Washington military field. A glance at its silhouette against the sky was enough. He knew instantly that it was Curly Brooks' all-blue plane.

Just why he did it, he did not stop to reason out at the moment. He simply spun the wave-length dial to Curly's S.O.S. reading.

"Curly, Curly!" he bellowed. "Go down and land! Go down and land at once. Anywhere—but for God's sake land!"

"For what?" came Brooks' calm voice. "Why...."

"I don't know!" Dusty cut him off frantically. "But just land, kid. For the love of God, land! I'll explain...."

He finished the rest with a bellow of alarm. Curly's plane seemed to suddenly stop dead in the air. Then it leaped crazily to one side, and through horrified eyes Dusty saw the left lower wing tear off and go flip-flopping away like so much crumpled tinfoil.

But at the same instant he saw a faint blur go streaking heavenward. At least he thought he saw a blur. He tried to follow it with his eyes, and saw nothing but blue sky.

Snapping his eyes back to Curly's ship he pounded the throttle with his free fist and cursed the Flash onto greater speed. Brooks' wingless ship was pivoting about slowly, like a leaf caught in the outer rim of a whirlpool. Faster and faster it moved, until it was plunging down in a tight spin.

"Out, Curly! Bail out—bail out!"

Dusty's roaring words echoed back to him dully, as he clawed air toward the spinning ship. As he neared it he saw Brooks struggling to shove himself up through the opened cowling. The pilot's movements were painfully slow.

He was like a half drowned man fumbling for a grip on a floating log. Three times he almost pulled himself clear, only to fall back into the cockpit again.

"Make it, Curly!" Dusty bellowed, as he circled helplessly about the other plane. "You've got to make it! Out—out! Bail out!"

It was evident that Curly was injured. Swinging in close, Dusty clearly saw the stream of blood that seeped out of a jagged gash on Brooks' left temple. Whether Curly knew he was there or not, was impossible to tell. The man was only half conscious and too occupied trying to pry himself out of his death trap.

Groaning and cursing in the same breath, Dusty followed his doomed pal lower and lower. The ground was sweeping up relentlessly, and Brooks was still wedged in the cockpit. And then, as though his brain had cleared a bit, the lean pilot heaved himself up with a tremendous effort.

Both hands digging and clawing at the turtle back of the

fuselage he managed to pull himself clear. A sudden whip of the plane hurled him to the side and off into the air.

Dusty shouted with joy, but groaned in the next breath. As Curly went flying off the tail swung around, and the rudder smashed into him. Like a sack of meal Brooks arced outward, and Dusty saw his pal drop like a stone.

"Pull it, pull it, Curly!" he thundered. "Pull the ring cord!"

But down Brooks went, his arms and legs spread-eagled in the air. Dusty raced down after him. A thousand feet from the ground Brooks was still falling like a lump of lead. Nine hundred—eight—seven—six....

"Curly! Curly, old pal!"

AT FOUR hundred a puff of white shot up from Curly's back. Dusty breathed a fierce prayer of thankfulness as 'chute silk mushroomed out, shroud lines went taut, and Curly's limp body was seemingly jerked back toward the sky for a moment.

"Knew you would, knew you would!" mumbled Dusty thickly, as he eased back the throttle. "You're just too tough, that's all!"

Swinging around in easy circles he watched Brooks float down the rest of the way. The lean pilot hit on the edge of a small wood, feet first. His knees buckled and he fell over on his face. Like a shroud the 'chute silk deflated on top of him.

Even as his pal hit, Dusty was cutting down to a quick fish-tail landing in a small field less than sixty yards away. The instant the wheels touched he cut the throttle and switch and leaped out.

Head down, fists clenched, he pounded over to the heap of 'chute silk flapping in a slight ground wind. Yanking it out of the way, he unbuckled the harness and rolled Curly over on his back.

As he did, the lean pilot's eyes fluttered open. They gaped dully at Dusty for a moment, then lighted up with recognition.

"The roof fell in, didn't it?"

Dusty grinned.

"Something like that, kid," he said happily. "How's it go? Think you can sit up? Here, use this."

As Brooks struggled to a sitting position, Dusty handed him his handkerchief. Curly groaned a bit and dabbed the handkerchief against his cut temple.

"The top of my head's gone," he grunted. "But outside of that, I'm swell. What happened? Something ran into me."

Dusty leaned forward.

"Did you see what it was?" he asked.

Curly blinked and shook his head.

"Hell, no! Didn't see anything. If I had, I'd have cut out of the way. But, listen—you yelled for me to land. Why? Didn't you—"

The look on Dusty's face stopped him.

"You didn't see anything?" he demanded. "Not even what smacked me?"

"Not a thing, kid," said Dusty.

And then he proceeded to tell Brooks of all that had happened.

"It was the Hawk all right," he finished up. "But how, and what the hell, I don't know!"

Curly fumbled for cigarettes, gave one to Dusty, and held

the match for them both. For a couple of minutes they smoked in silence. Presently, Curly cursed and snapped his half-smoked cigarette away.

"I've seen a few tough ones in my time!" he grunted, staring off into space. But this takes the cake, and how! You hear the guy, and you feel what he does—but you don't see him. Hell, he must have been pulling a bluff about that Federal Building. Sure you didn't see any explosion? Black Agents might have bombed it, you know."

Dusty shook his head.

"The explosion was afterward," he said firmly. "After the building caved in. I'm sure of that. I happened to be looking at it, right at that moment. The front and back sides seemed to cave in in the center. Between the fiftieth and sixtieth floors. Then the rest of it came down in a shower of steel and stone."

"Bombs could do that," said Curly doggedly.

"Right! But they didn't. The same thing that got the cruisers, spilled me and damn near wiped you out, also got the Federal Building. It must have, don't you see? The Hawk called the turn on every damn thing that happened!"

Curly dabbed the handkerchief to his temple and heaved a sigh of complete puzzlement.

"Maybe you're right," he grunted. "And if so—what a sweet war this is turning out to be! Can't even see a guy when he smacks you. Oh well, maybe this is life. Anyway, where do we go from here? You want me to walk back to the drome, now?"

Dusty gave him the hard eye.

"If you'd done as I told you," he snapped, "instead of sneaking back, you'd have saved me a few gray hairs!"

"And some of my own!" nodded Brooks. "Sorry. I guess I'm too curious at times."

"Forget it, kid," grinned Dusty, jabbing him playfully in the ribs. "We're both alive, and that's what counts. Come on. There's a road near here. We'll get you a lift to the military field, and I'll fly my crate back."

"The chauffeur's on his way," said Curly, getting to his feet. "Take a look."

Dusty turned to see a staff car come tearing around the far end of the wood and spray dirt toward them. As it skidded to a full stop a burly figure in uniform leaped out of the rear seat. It was General Horner. He advanced on them with blazing eyes, which he finally fastened on Dusty.

"Hell of a way to obey orders, Ayres!" he boomed. "I've been expecting you for hours!"

"Sorry, sir," began Dusty. "But I—"

"Never mind, now," the other cut him off. "Get into the back of the car—both of you!"

Dusty hesitated, glanced at his plane.

"Brooks will ride with you, sir," he said. "I'll fly the ship back, and meet—"

"Get into the car!" General Horner thundered. "Leave the plane here. The field crew will pick it up. I don't think you'll be needing it for a while. Get in!"

Dusty shot him a questioning glance, shrugged and followed Curly into the car.

43

CHAPTER 4
FIRE-EYES

S LUMPED BACK against the cushions Dusty shot quick side glances at General Horner as they raced, siren wailing, through the streets of the Nation's Capitol. The Intelligence chief was staring straight ahead, unblinking. His face was set in grim lines, and his hands resting on his lap were bunched into hammerhead fists.

A dozen times Dusty was on the point of asking questions, but each time he curbed the impulse. Knowing General Horner of old, he realized that the man would talk when the time was ready, and not a split second before. He was like that—so was his son, Agent 10.

Resigned to the inevitable, Dusty contented himself with mulling over his own thoughts. That the Blacks had brought into play some new, mysterious and terrible weapon of war was a foregone conclusion.

Too many things had happened, to be taken as coincidence. As he had told Curly, the same thing—whatever in God's name it was—had done all the damage. And the Hawk was behind it all. No need of giving that truth a second thought. But—how?

How could the Hawk destroy three powerful battle cruisers in as many minutes? How could the Hawk, high in the air, crumple the towering Federal Building into flaming ruins? How could the Hawk fling his own ship out of control? And how could that devil rip Curly's wings clean off? But, even more important—how could the Hawk do all those things and still be invisible?

Dusty's brain raced backward in memory. He thought of Pilot Vance's last words. The navyman had spoken of yellow lightning. What had he meant by that? Was it possible that the Blacks were able to discharge great bolts of lightning from great distances, and regulate where they would strike? Hell, that was absurd—preposterous! Yet—he'd seen something. Just a blur—or maybe had just an hallucination of the retina. At any rate, he was positive that it was not colored. If it was a blur, it was grey-black.

"Out, gentlemen!"

Horner's voice jerked Dusty back to the present. The car had slid to a gentle stop in front of the War Department Building, and a ram-rod sergeant guard was holding open the car door.

Climbing out he waited for Curly and General Horner, and then with his pal followed the Intelligence Chief up the broad stone steps and into the elevator lobby. As though it had all been planned ahead of time, the very first elevator was empty save for the operator and an armed guard.

With a nod of his head, General Horner motioned them inside, and got in himself. The doors clicked shut and the car shot fifty-seven stories skyward.

The doors clicked open again as the car stopped. General Horner nodded his head again and stepped out into a long corridor. A guard, pacing slowly up and down, stiffened to attention and saluted.

Horner didn't even notice him. In long strides, he moved

down the corridor, through a door at the end, and down a shorter corridor to another door. Dusty knew where they were headed for he had been in the place several times before. They were headed for Horner's private office.

He glanced at Curly, keeping step at his side, and grinned. The lean pilot frowned and formed unspoken questions with his lips. Dusty shrugged and gestured complete ignorance.

AS THEY passed through the last door they entered a large office, conspicuous for its lack of furniture and for its rows of file cases that literally covered the lower part of all four walls. Horner seated himself behind a huge desk, jerked a thumb at a couple of nearby vacant chairs, and punched one of a row of buzzer buttons that lined the right side of his desk.

Almost immediately a side door opened and a young Medical Corps lieutenant stepped inside. He carried a small black case in his right hand. General Horner flashed him a look and nodded at Curly Books.

"Fix up that officer's wound," he ordered.

And then as though totally unaware of the existence of anybody else in the room he fell to frowning and fuming over a pile of papers on his desk. Not until the medico had patched up Curly's gashed temple and had left the room, did he look tip. And then he fixed narrowed eyes on Dusty.

"The whole story, right from the beginning, Ayres, please," he ordered. Then added, a trifle tartly, "That is, if there is a beginning."

Dusty gave him eye for eye for a moment, sucked in his breath slowly, and then proceeded to tell his story for the second time in as many hours. Horner listened through to the end in savage frowning silence. And when Dusty stopped, he glanced at Curly.

"Anything to add to that, Lieutenant?" he rapped out.

Brooks shook his head.

"Nothing, sir," he said. "Except that I only heard Dusty's first conversation with the Hawk. I didn't hear any more, although I kept my set open on S.O.S. Emergency all of the time."

"The answer to that is simple enough," grunted Horner. "The Blacks have perfected a new directional transmission beam that is insulated against all attempts of other stations to listen in. He probably used the regular wave at first."

"Then that's—" began Dusty.

"How he got those cruisers to go to M Twenty-Four, without our knowing it?" the senior officer cut in. "Exactly! And at the same time our efforts to contact them were blanketed out—right here in the Navy H.Q. station!"

Dusty started.

"Huh, sir?"

The general gestured irritably.

"One of their agents!" he said shortly. "Only caught the rat a few hours ago. Fixed it so that Navy H.Q. radio was simply transmitting right back into its own receivers."

"But wait a minute," Dusty interrupted. "Collins at my own field picked up that message sent to the cruisers. If there was a directional beam used, why—?"

"I know what you're getting at," Horner stopped him. "And

I've only got one answer. It was sent direct to your field, for your benefit!"

"My benefit?" echoed Dusty.

"I think so," nodded the other. "It was to dove-tail in with that unsigned message you got from the Hawk—so that you would be sure to be at M Twenty-Four. At least that's the way I figured it, after Major Drake told me about the radio to you."

SILENCE SETTLED over the room as Horner stopped talking. Eyes brittle and fixed on the desk top, the Intelligence chief sat rigid slowly clenching and unclenching his hands. Dusty stood it for a few minutes, then leaned forward.

"Any idea of what's back of it, sir?" he encouraged.

Horner snapped his head up, glared at him.

"Back of it?" he echoed harshly. "Of course I have. It's an attempt to cripple us by smashing down from the top!"

Dusty frowned.

"I don't think I get you."

"Do you know who was on the *Texas?*" General Horner asked sharply.

"No, sir."

"Then I'll tell you. The *Texas* carried the Secretary of the Navy, the Assistant Secretary, and Admiral Trenton of the Atlantic Battle Fleet. Those three, and half a dozen lesser lights. They selected the *Texas* as a good place to confer and make plans regarding the blockading of Canadian ports of both coasts. A lot of the Blacks' equipment is coming from their captured territories in Europe and Asia. They couldn't possibly keep going on what's left in Canada. So we've been contemplating a starving-out blockade on all materials. And now—"

Horner paused and shrugged.

"And now the keymen of the plan are at the bottom of the Atlantic!" he growled.

"More Black agent work, eh?" murmured Dusty. Then as an after thought, "But, gosh, with the Secretary aboard would they still carry out an order from U.S.N. Twelve? I should think that they—"

"That's just how clever these damn Blacks plan things!" the senior officer stopped him short. "In addition to the conference, the Secretary and the others were going to witness trials of a new-type gun just recently installed. To do it in actual battle against a light force would be perfect. See what I mean? Those devils didn't miss a bet."

Dusty nodded sympathetically, but made no comment. He could fully realize just how General Horner felt. As Chief of Intelligence the criticism of all Black agent activity in the U.S. descended upon him. Added to that he was personally responsible for the activities of the vast number of U.S. secret agents under his command. As Dusty had often said to himself, of all the jobs in the Army, the Navy and the Air Force, General Horner's job was the last one he'd choose.

"And to add to that," spoke up Horner again. "As near as I can learn, they have wiped out practically half of the General Staff!"

"They were aboard too?" gasped Curly Brooks.

"Hell no!" the general flung at him. "They were in the Federal

Building in Boston, attending a Northeastern Area council of war."

In spite of himself, Dusty turned and glanced at the row of windows on his right. The general saw his action and grunted.

"Don't blame you a bit, Ayres," he said. "I've had my eye on them ever since we came in. By God, any more of this, and I think I'll lose my mind. It's incredible, absolutely impossible— yet it's fact!"

Dusty's eyes narrowed, as he realized that the big moment was coming.

"What's fact, sir?" he asked in tensed tone.

General Horner didn't answer at once. He sat scowling at his folded hands on the desk-top, as though choosing his words before he spoke them. When he did they came out slowly— almost reluctant to leave his lips.

"The Blacks have a new weapon of war, the name of which when translated from their language means, The Red Destroyer. What it is, I do not know. After what's happened, I'm pretty positive that it is some kind of an air weapon—something invisible to the human eye. But that they have a new weapon is positive fact. Here, this is a translated report from Agent Ten."

DUSTY ACCEPTED the sheet of paper that the other passed him, absently noting the fact for the hundredth time that General Horner never spoke of his own son by any other name than his official one—Agent 10. He glanced at the paper; held it so that Curly could read it, too.

X to X-34

New weapon titled the Red Destroyer perfected by Blacks for early use. Nature and design not known. Expect to obtain complete details within twenty-four hours. Will send them through the same channels.

X

Placing the paper on the desk, Dusty looked at General Horner.

"Mind telling me where Jack sent that from, sir?" he asked. "And when?"

The other shook his head.

"Not at all," he said. "Agent 10 sent that from Halifax yesterday noon."

"Halifax?" grunted Dusty. "What was Jack doing up there?"

General Horner gave him a scornful look.

"My agents follow down every rumor," he said simply. "And unless I miss my guess, Agent 10 has caught on to something rather important."

The senior officer paused and glanced at his watch. As he raised his eyes he saw the questioning look on Dusty's face.

"If I'm lucky," he muttered. "We'll hear from Agent 10 in about fifteen minutes. You two follow me."

With that General Horner stood up and walked out of the office. Silently Dusty and Curly followed him out and through the corridors to the elevator. On the seventy-ninth floor they got off, walked down a long steel-walled corridor and entered a dimly lighted room at the far end. As Dusty stepped through the door a tingling thrill rippled through him. Months before, he had been in this very room, and had heard the President deliver his answer to the impossible ultimatum of Fire-Eyes.

The room had not changed, save for the possible addition of more instruments. Instinctively Dusty's eyes went to the south wall. He sucked in his breath sharply as he saw the Telerad screen on the wall. On that screen he had first seen the televisioned picture of the high commander of the Black Invaders.

"Well, captain, a lot of water has passed under the bridge since we last met."

Dusty turned to stare into the grinning features of Major Jordon, chief radio officer at Washington H.Q. They had first met in that very room on the day war had been declared. He grasped the other's hand and shook it warmly.

"Yes, sir," he said, "a whole lot. And it looks like more to come."

Major Jordon's face went grave. He nodded his head slowly.

"I'm afraid so," he said. "Very much afraid so."

As though there were nothing more to say, Jordon turned away and walked over to the dial panel on the north wall, where General Horner stood waiting, an impatient look on his rugged face.

"Any contact, yet, Jordon?" boomed out the Intelligence chief. The radio officer shook his head.

"No, sir," he said. "I've been trying at ten minute intervals— but no luck yet."

General Horner glared at the instrument panel a moment, then fell to pacing slowly up and down the length of the room. Dusty stepped in front of him on the fifth time down.

"Pardon, sir. Supposing you don't contact Agent 10. Then what?"

The senior officer fixed him with a steady eye.

"What do you mean, Ayres?"

Dusty shrugged.

"They're already using the Red Destroyer, sir," he said. "I'd suggest, sir, that we take steps, ourselves, to find out what it is and track it down, just in case we don't hear from Agent 10."

The other grunted.

"And just what do you suggest we do?" he asked.

Dusty hesitated, stared at the floor a moment.

"Well, sir," he began, "our first job is to find out what it is. We both believe it's some kind of an air weapon. Assuming that it is, why not arrange for it to be at a certain place so that we can get a look at it."

"Arrange for it to be at a certain place?" boomed back General Horner. "Have you gone out of your head, Ayres? Just what the devil do you mean?"

"This, sir," Dusty replied calmly. "Let us make the Blacks believe that—"

"General Horner!"

The sharp exclamation from Major Jordon cut off the rest Dusty was about to say. The Intelligence chief spun away from him and over to the radio officer. Dusty followed at his heels. And Curly Brooks was close behind.

"Yes, Jordon? What is it?"

"Some one is trying to get through to us, sir," replied the radio officer pointing at a quivering needle on a dial in front of him. "And, I think it's our secret Telerad station just outside Halifax."

"Think?" General Horner barked at him. "Good God, man, don't you know? Can't you find out?"

A look of annoyance flashed across Major Jordon's face and faded away almost instantly. He reached out and twirled one or two dials.

"Can't say for sure, yet, sir," he said in even tone of voice. "It may just be a bit of local disturbance."

General Horner snorted but said nothing. And in silence they all watched Major Jordon work on the dial knobs.

Presently he stiffened, pressed a receiving phone against his ear and listened intently. Breath clamped in his lungs, Dusty watched him intently. His heart was pounding against his ribs, and the blood surging through his veins. At any minute now, they might see Jack Horner on the Telerad screen, and hear his voice as he spoke his important message.

But an instant later he groaned inwardly. Major Jordon had relaxed, had taken the phone away from his ear, and was shaking his head sadly.

"Almost had it that time!" he muttered as though talking to himself. "Dammit! Wonder what's the matter? Some one must be on the other end!"

FACE GRIM he set to work on the dials again. As he turned one, a high keyed hum filled the room. It mounted and mounted until it faded off to nothing. Instantly Major Jordon clipped a transmitter speaking tube about his neck, and started flipping down a series of relay switches and jamming contact plugs into

"DAMMIT! WONDER WHATS THE MATTER? SOME ONE MUST BE ON THE OTHER END!"

their sockets. As he did so he shot a quick triumphant glance at General Horner.

"Got it this time, sir!" he snapped.

Horner nodded, and said nothing. Major Jordon turned back to the dial board, put his lips to the transmitter tube.

"H-Six, H-Six!" he called. "Signals coming through very weak. Try four-nine-ten, or seven-two-five! Can you hear me H-Six?"

As the radio officer stopped talking, the high-keyed hum returned. Then it faded away again and from out of the panel speaker unit came a throaty mumble of unintelligible sounds. Jordon cursed, regardless of the presence of his superior officer, and fiddled frantically with the dials. And presently the mumble of sound became clearly spoken words.

"... A on twelve-four-eight, Washington H.Q. There is cut-in frequency disturbance at this end. Try twelve-four-eight, Washington H.Q."

"We hear you all right, H-Six!" Jordon shouted into the transmitter tube. "Go ahead. Switch over to Telerad power. We are ready!"

As one man they all turned and stared at the silver Telerad screen in its oblong frame on the south wall. Faint wavy lines of light were beginning to ripple across its surface, from left to right. Faster and faster they moved. A moment later other lines of light started waving down front top to bottom. At the same instant an eerie hissing sound came out from the screen.

But presently, though, the hissing sound faded into oblivion. The lines moved even faster until finally the whole screen seemed to be covered by a sheet of clear white flame. And then from out of its center there came clicking sound that slowly merged into a human voice.

"H-Six switching in, Washington H.Q. Am I registering clearly?"

Dusty, his eyes riveted to the screen heard Major Jordon click down a couple of switches, and speak into the transmitter tube.

"Coming through H-Six! You are registering. Swing on full volume slowly. Doing it at this end!"

"Swinging on full volume, Washington!" intoned the voice from out of the center of the Telerad screen.

As the last died away to the echo, the screen darkened a bit. Shadows flickered across it, and flickered back again. Then, suddenly they stopped and became motionless. Gradually, like the developing of a photographic film, they took on shapes and clear outlines of the head and shoulders of a man. The figure itself, remained dark for a moment. Then it began to clear too. And in the matter of perhaps five seconds the picture became perfectly clear.

"My God, it's Fire-Eyes!"

Dusty hardly heard General Horner's wild shout. Rooted to the spot, he stood like a man in a trance, gaping open-mouthed at the green mask and blazing orbs of the commander-in-chief of the Black Invaders!

CHAPTER 5
DEATH TO THE NORTH

"YES, GENERAL Horner, it is I, Fire-Eyes, emperor of the world! You were expecting to see your son, Agent 10, were you not?"

"Damn your soul!" roared the Intelligence chief. "I'll—I'll—"

A mocking laugh from behind the green mask cut off the rest.

Trembling with rage, General Horner raised one clenched fist, as though he were actually going to smash it against the screen on the wall. So sure was Dusty that the general was going to strike, that he reached over and grabbed the senior officer's arm.

Horner jerked his arm free, glared at him, then suddenly relaxed.

"Sorry, Ayres," he muttered. "Thanks."

Dusty grinned, and turned his eyes back to the Telerad screen. The head and shoulders of the Black commander-in-chief were still clearly visible. Dusty glanced at it, then on sudden impulse, turned and walked over to the transmission recording plate on the dial panel.

"What's the answer this time, Fire-Eyes?" he grated into the speaking tube just under the plate.

By turning his head he could, see the Telerad screen. The black-hooded green mask was bobbing up and down, and a harsh chuckle was rolling out from the center of the screen.

"Ah, the great Captain Ayres, I believe! It is a shame that we meet at such a great distance."

"That's your fault!" Dusty clipped back at him. "We might get together, if you didn't hole up so often. Why didn't you hang around the Chihuahua Hills a little longer, a couple of weeks ago? I would have been back."

Strange sounds came from the Telerad screen. Dusty guessed that Fire-Eyes was swearing in his native language. He made a mental note to learn that language some day—it always sounded so absolutely cockeyed and crazy.

And then the Black spoke again.

"Let me remind you, captain, that our memory is long. In fact, we Blacks never forget."

"Like elephants, huh?" Dusty broke in on him.

"Exactly!" the other roared. "And our strength—when revenge is ours—thrice as great. You speak of the Chihuahua Hills—what you saw there were but mere experiments. Now, we have reached the stage of perfection. Ah, no, not in the way you think. That Strato-plane is history. The Red Destroyer has taken its place. Today, you yourself saw what it could do. That, captain, was but practice!"

The voice from the screen stopped abruptly, and the green mask with its blazing orbs nodded vigorously. Despite the eerie tingle that rippled up and down his spine, Dusty grinned and snorted scornfully.

"That's what you think!" he rapped out. "Why not practice some more? You may be surprised. I—"

Dusty stopped short as steel fingers gripped his arm and

pressed hard. He turned to stare into General Horner's flushed face. The Intelligence chief was shaking his head savagely, and holding a silencing finger to his lips.

"You fool, Ayres!" the senior officer hissed softly, yet angrily. "Do you want more of us killed? We've got to find out what it is, first!"

On the spur of the moment, Dusty gave him the agate eye; pulled his arm free.

"What the devil do you think I'm trying to do?" he breathed fiercely, totally forgetful of rank.

And then before General Horner had a chance to say anything, he turned back to the speaker unit.

"How about it, Fire-Eyes?" he asked. "Calling my bluff? It is a bluff, of course."

The figure on the screen remained silent and completely motionless for a minute. Then words came out from behind the mask—harsh, grating words, filled with obvious contempt.

"Your views and your comments matter nothing to me, Captain Ayres! If General Horner has recovered from the shock, put him back on registering contact, please."

DUSTY HAD nothing to do about it. General Horner grabbed him and virtually hurled him away from the transmitting screen. Chagrined, Dusty grinned at Curly. His pal did not grin back. In fact, there was an expression of marked disapproval on his face. Major Jordon also shared the same expression. Dusty shrugged and let his eyes bore absently into the back of General Horner's neck.

The Intelligence chief was clearing his throat, and about to speak.

"Am I registering, Fire-Eyes? If so, speak your piece. I'm in a hurry. I have other things to do."

A booming, derisive laugh came from the screen to mock the words.

"Are they more important than the fate of your son, General Horner?"

Dusty saw his senior officer stiffen, and then slowly relax. When Horner spoke again his voice was steady, almost flat and entirely without emotion.

"My son is a soldier, Fire-Eyes. If he is dead, he died a brave and loyal American. If he lives, he lives to blast you and your slaughtering hordes from the face of the earth. Now what is it you wish to say to me?"

The green mask seemed to grow bigger. It was as though the Black Commander were leaning closer to the recording plate at the other end of the Telerad wave-length.

"I give you a message to take to your President and Congressional Committee!" boomed Fire-Eyes. "Yes, in fact, it is a message for the entire American nation."

The voice stopped abruptly. The silence that followed was so heavy that Dusty swore that he could actually hear his own heart beat.

"And that message?" asked General Horner.

"This!" replied the voice on the Telerad screen. "That your forces and mine declare a two months' armistice, during which time our selected delegations will meet and discuss terms of peace."

Had Fire-Eyes himself dropped through the steel roof of the radio room at that moment, Dusty would not have been more surprised. The words of the Black commander echoed and re-echoed about inside his head. Discuss terms of peace? Fire-Eyes wanted peace? Like hell he did! The murdering devil was up—

General Horner was talking.

"And what assurance have we that you would maintain an armistice? It would not be the first time that you and your breed have gone back on your word."

"You have the same assurance of what I will do, that I have of what you will do!" the Black boomed back at him.

"And if I refuse?" asked General Horner calmly. "If we refuse because of what you have done today?"

The screen was silent for perhaps ten seconds. And then the voice of Satan, himself, came forth.

"You cannot and dare not refuse! If you do, what has happened today will be as nothing. Every ship of yours that floats will be sent to the bottom—just as were the *Texas, Utah* and *Vermont.* Every building in your national capital will be reduced to smouldering ruins. Your entire government will be crushed into the earth. And when we have done that, we shall proceed to gain additional revenge upon a population fools enough to permit greater fools to guide their destinies.

"Should you deem to take these words lightly, General Horner, think of what happened today. Even Captain Ayres, who saw a demonstration, is as ignorant of it all as you and all the others.

I assure you, it was no accident—it was accomplished with a definite purpose. That of forewarning you of events to come, should you refuse my request."

"And you have no terms of peace now?" put in General Horner as the voice paused. "Once you delivered an ultimatum, but now you request that selected delegations meet. That leads me to suspect weakness-a weakening on your part, Fire-Eyes. And I believe that the President and Congressional Committee will undoubtedly suspect the same thing."

The Black commander-in-chief laughed harshly. So much

so, in fact, that his large green mask seemed to actually quiver. And presently he spoke.

"Let you, or anyone else, General Horner, think what they may! You have my request, and you have my warning if it is not fulfilled. Take it before those in power in your country. I give you twenty-four hours in which to answer. If you have not done so by this time tomorrow, let the results be on your head. We will—."

At that instant the Telerad screen gave forth the clear, sharp sound of a pistol shot. Through startled eyes, Dusty saw the figure of Fire-Eyes jerk backward. One black gauntleted hand rose into view, then dropped back out of sight again. An unintelligible roar came from behind the green mask. Fire-Eyes seemed to half turn. And then he faded from view as the Telerad screen darkened, and thin wavy lines of light rippled across its surface.

"Jordon, Jordon! Tune it in clearer—in clearer! We've got to see what happened!"

GENERAL HORNER'S voice filled the steel- and copper-paneled radio room like the thunder of heavy cannonading. Out the corner of his eye, Dusty saw the radio officer leap for the wall dial panel and work feverishly with relay switches and volume dials. But it was all to no avail.

The thin wavy lines of light moved slower and slower. Presently there was a half hissing, half wailing sound, and the Telerad screen changed to its original silvery appearance. Jordon's savage curse broke the two or three seconds of silence.

"No use!" he grated. "It's at the other end. Something went

wrong. Power cut off. H-Six isn't even registering a single degree on the dial."

The man spoke as though to himself. And the others hardly heard him. Like statues of stone they stood gaping at the blank Telerad screen—the same question burning through every brain.

"That was a shot, or I'm a liar!" suddenly spoke up Curly Brooks.

If nothing, it served to snap the tension. General Horner half turned, fixed him with blazing scornful eyes.

"Of course it was!" he boomed. "It didn't sound like a baby crying, did it?" And then in a low mumble, "What does it mean? By God, what does it mean?"

"I can make a good guess," Dusty put in quietly.

"Oh, you can, can you?" the senior officer whirled on him. "Something as bright as your fool remarks to Fire-Eyes, I suppose?"

Dusty's jaw came out and his shoulders went back.

"Yes, sir," he said evenly. "Equally as bright. That shot was the answer to a question that you've been asking yourself a thousand times in the last ten minutes, I'll wager."

General Horner scowled at him, walked over and stood regarding him, arms akimbo.

"And just what in the devil do you mean by that?" he snapped out.

"I mean that Agent 10 must still be alive!" Dusty shot right back at him. "I admit it's guess work—but I'm guessing that Agent 10 tried to wing Fire-Eyes. And—and didn't make out so good. Otherwise, we would have seen Fire-Eyes drop immediately."

General Horner's face paled a bit, and some of the blazing anger seeped out of his eyes.

"God, I wonder if you're right?" he breathed softly. "But—but why should he when Fire-Eyes was asking for a peace discussion? Killing Fire-Eyes would probably only stop the rest of the Blacks temporarily."

"Why should he?" echoed Dusty. "I'll tell you why. Because Agent 10 knows what I'm guessing—that Fire-Eyes' peace and armistice talk is a lot of crab apples. That big tramp doesn't want peace, any more than I want to wear skirts! It's a stall for something. Jack—Agent 10—got wise to it, and took a crack at Fire-Eyes in an effort to hold up the parade even longer. I—"

Dusty stopped abruptly, stared hard at the floor. General Horner reached out and touched his arm.

"Go on, Ayres," he said. "Finish it!"

The pilot didn't look up.

"I'm only hoping and praying that Jack got away again," he said in a low voice.

There was silence for a moment, during which time Dusty wished that he'd bitten off his tongue instead of saying those words. Presently he looked up and met Horner's eyes.

"You thought I'd gone off my nut a while ago, sir," he said. "But I did have an idea. Mind if I do a bit more talking?"

The senior officer hesitated, and shook his head.

"Go ahead and talk," he said thickly, evident hopelessness in his voice. "That seems to be the only thing that any of us can do right now."

"Oh, no, it isn't sir," Dusty came back at him quickly. "There is—"

He broke off short, shot an inquiring glance at Major Jordon.

"Any sets open, major?" he asked. "I don't want my words to go out of this room under any circumstances!"

"That would be impossible," the radio officer assured him firmly. "The whole place is sound-proof, and there isn't a single contact wave-length open. Take a look for yourself."

He waved a hand toward the dial panel. Dusty glanced that way and noted that every dial needle was hard up against the zero peg. He nodded with satisfaction and switched his eyes back to General Horner's frowning face.

"We admit that we're walking in circles, sir, right now. Isn't that correct?"

"Frankly, it is."

"We also admit that the Blacks have some new weapon, more terrible than anything else they've brought out so far. Correct?"

"Yes," impatiently.

"And we don't know what it is, or where it is—or what to do about it. Right?"

General Horner cursed softly.

"Yes, yes, yes, Ayres! Get on with it. I admit everything you say. Now, just what the devil are you driving at?"

DUSTY RAISED his hands, palms, upward, stared hard at them a minute or two, then linked the fingers together and squeezed tightly.

"Our first task," he spoke slowly, "is to get a good look at the thing—whatever it is. And, not knowing where it's going to strike next, it's our best bet to arrange for it to strike where we want it to strike."

"You said something like that before," cut in the Intelligence chief. "Just before Fire-Eyes came on the Telerad."

"I know!" Dusty answered him sharply. "I had the idea then. That's why I spoke as I did to Fire-Eyes. Now, think back to the Chihuahua show. Remember that X-Rayoscope of Major Trapp's? That new gadget that allowed one to see the ground from a good eighty-six thousand through clouds or darkness of night? And the two built were destroyed? Remember?"

"Naturally, I do," nodded Horner. "And a new one has already been constructed."

"Yeah, I know," grinned Dusty. "Since we lost those two, I've been hankering to try one out. I kept in touch with Major Trapp while I was still in the Hospital. The third one is all ready for testing. As a matter of fact I have a tentative date with the Major to try it out some time tomorrow."

"Yes, yes," said General Horner, again growing impatient. "I believe that Trapp mentioned something about it to me last evening. But what's that got to do with the job that confronts us now?"

"Everything," replied Dusty calmly. "The X-Rayoscope has a vision range—a magnified vision range—of a good three hundred miles, from sea level up to eighty-six thousand feet. That, by the way, is Major Trapp's report on this third model. Now, here is the point, sir."

Dusty paused, licked his lower lip, and looked straight into the other's eyes.

"By methods best known to yourself," he said, "you can get the word spread about that there is to be a special conference of Intelligence Staff, and Washington H.Q. Staff, in the old War College Building over in Alexandria. Now, it's such an important and secret conference that you're going to hold it at early dawn tomorrow. Say, five o'clock. But, naturally, nobody is going to attend. You are just to see that the secret slips out- enough for a couple of Black agents to scoop it up. See?"

Horner shook his head vigorously.

"I certainly don't!" he grunted, "What will be the good of all that tommy-rot?"

Dusty sighed and shrugged.

"That remains to be seen, sir," he said evenly. "But the Blacks smashed up a naval confab at sea, and an Army Staff confab in the Federal building. So, it's my guess that they'd leap at the chance to do the same thing to an Intelligence and Washington Staff confab in the old War College Building."

"I get it, kid!" cried Curly excitedly. "I get—!"

Dusty silenced him with a frown, glanced questioningly at General Horner. The Intelligence chief was nodding slowly.

"I think I begin to get it, too, Ayres. Go on."

"Losing the War College building, won't bother us, sir," continued Dusty. "It hasn't been used for years. Now, Curly and I will take the X-Rayoscope ship up around midnight, hang up at maximum altitude and keep the lens trained on the War College building. The rest will be a cinch—we'll see what the damn thing is, where it goes, etc. Then we'll hike after it—and begin from scratch to wipe it out."

Dusty finished with a questioning gesture. General Horner stared fixedly at him, lips pressed together in a thin line.

"It sounds possible, to hear you tell it, Ayres," he nodded presently. "But, supposing you lose it—and can't find it. Then what? You heard what Fire-Eyes said? God, it gives me the creeps to think of what several of those damn things could do—whatever in the devil's name it is!"

"By God, you hit it, sir! That's it, to be sure!"

General Horner's mouth jerked open.

"Huh? What the hell do you mean?"

Dusty smashed a clenched fist into the palm of the other hand.

"Don't you see, sir?" he cried. "It's the reason for the two months armistice peace stall. This new weapon of his is hell on wheels—but, he's only got *one of them!* It's my hunch that he wants two months of peace in which to concentrate on turning out enough of them to wipe us clean off the map in one fell swoop. Hell, our lines up north are giving his troops plenty to think about. Their supplies are running low—so you believe. O.K., two months for him to turn out this new weapon in quantities, and he'll be set to continue the offensive war he's been waging, right from the start!

And the idea of what happened today, was to throw a scare into us, so that we'd agree to a two months' armistice, at least. As for Curly and I being successful—well, we can only hope like hell for the best. At any rate, as I see it, sir, it's our only bet—and our best one."

Whether or not he was conscious of what he was doing, General Horner half turned and stared at Major Jordon. The radio office nodded slightly.

"I agree with Captain Ayres, sir," he said quietly. "It seems to be our best bet."

A long sigh slid off the Intelligence chief's lips. He turned his eyes back to Dusty's face.

"I guess you're right, Ayres," he said gruffly. "Very well, I'll see that the Blacks get hold of a fake order. Anything else you suggest?"

Dusty grinned, and shook his head.

"Nothing, sir," he said. "Except, that you might keep all official wave-lengths open from quarter to five on. And—thanks. Come on, Curly! We'll tuck some food in, and then go to work."

The last was unnecessary. Curly Brooks, a mile-wide eager smile on his lips was already waiting, his hand on the knob of the radio room door.

CHAPTER 6
THE HURTLING DOOM

A THIN crescent moon was hanging low down on the southern horizon as Dusty, Curly Brooks, and Major Trapp stood smoking cigarettes on the edge of a small field buried deep in the heart of the Blue Ridge Mountains of Virginia.

Close by was a stubby-winged, barrel-shaped cabin biplane, with the telescopic projector of the X-Rayoscope unit sticking out through the slanting center glass window of the cabin. On secret orders, Major Trapp had flown the plane from the Air Force Experimental field at Indianapolis and landed not over an hour ago.

After a careful and detailed examination of the craft and its weird instrument that magnified objects to the human eye through fog, clouds and darkness of night from a height of eighty-six thousand feet and for a distance of over three hundred miles, Dusty and Curly were making a final check-up with its designer.

The hour was exactly eleven-forty five, and save for the faint, almost indistinct glow shed by the waning moon, the heavens were as dark as the bottom shaft of a coal mine.

"Keep your eye on the power dial," Major Trapp was warning. "It will help you regulate focus in case you are forced to change altitude. And one thing, more. For heaven's sake don't stunt the ship! It's not a pursuit job, and it's not built for that type of work. If you do, and the X-Rayoscope comes off its brackets and lands on you, you'll sure know it. By the way, there's a chute apiece for you, under the pilot's seat."

"I know, I saw them," nodded Dusty. And then with a rueful smile. "But, I wish I'd seen a couple of mounted Brownings, too. You never know what might happen. And I'm funny that way—I like to be prepared."

"I know you do," grinned Major Trapp. "But as I said, this is no pursuit job, and I'm hoping you're going to keep out of trouble."

Dusty shrugged.

"Well, here's hoping just in case," he said. Then turning to Curly, "It's getting late, kid, let's go."

After shaking hands with Major Trapp the two of them toed out their cigarettes, walked over to the plane and climbed in the cabin door.

"You take the controls, Curly," said Dusty as he seated himself behind the tripod-mounted X-Rayoscope.

Curly glared at him and dropped into the pilot's seat.

"You have everything, don't you sweetheart!" he snapped, and kicked the electric starter.

Two minutes later, without the aid of floodlights, Curly sent the plane racing across the small field, and zoomed it up into the night darkened skies.

Totally oblivious to his pal, Dusty stared absently at the X-Rayoscope regulating panel just to his left. The old familiar tingling sensation was rippling up and down his spine.

On the ground the job had seemed simple enough. All he had to do was to sight this new weapon of the Black Invaders, assuming, of course, that it was an aerial weapon, and follow it back to its base.

But now, as he thundered higher and higher into the night skies, doubt gripped him and flooded his brain with a hundred and one tantalizing thoughts.

WITH A muttered curse he brushed the thoughts from his brain and glanced at his watch. The hands showed exactly twenty minutes after twelve. A look at the altimeter needle told him that they were swinging up past the fifty-five thousand foot mark. Instinctively he marveled at the climbing performance of the plane, and calculated it as against his own Silver Flash. The result, as far as climbing performance was concerned, was in favor of the X-Rayoscope plane.

When, eventually, the altimeter needle reached eighty-five thousand feet, and Curly leveled off, he turned and grinned at his pal.

"Pretty good for a greenhorn," he said. "Now I'll take over."

Curly gave him the hard eye, shrugged and put the ship on robot control.

"And now what am I supposed To do?" He grunted, as they changed seats.

Dusty grinned.

"Just be a good little boy and don't ask questions," he said.

Checking his position on the roller map, he veered slightly northward, eased back the throttle, and sat staring at the tiny cowl lamp that illuminated the instrument board.

And then, suddenly, his attention was attracted to the red signal light on the radio panel. It was blinking rapidly. Shooting out his free hand he snapped on the set and spun the wave-length dial.

As the indicator reached the S.O.S. emergency reading a series of high-keyed sounds came blasting out of the earphones. He listened intently for a few seconds, then glanced at Curly who had half turned in his seat.

"Maybe I'm wrong," he said. "But I've a hunch that we're in

luck. Some Black station is shooting out a lot of stuff in their secret high speed code. If you ask me, some lad is relaying General Horner's fake order up to Black H.Q."

Curly made no comment. He simply shrugged his shoulders and turned forward again. Snapping off the set, Dusty checked his position on the roller map, and sent the plane drifting lazily about in a series of ever-widening circles.

The seconds raced by and became minutes. The minutes became hours, and eventually Dusty's radium dial watch showed exactly seventeen minutes of five.

As he glanced toward the east he could just faintly see the first rays of a new dawn seeping up over the Atlantic's horizon. Below him the ground was still blanketed in indistinguishable murkiness. Setting the controls on robot he heaved himself out of the seat, took a step forward and tapped Curly on the shoulder.

"Hold her as she goes, kid," he said. "I'll do the looking from now on."

Without a look or a single gesture Curly got up and moved back to the pilot's seat. Dropping into the seat that Curly had vacated, Dusty snapped on X-Rayoscope power and slowly turned the volume control knob. Hunching forward he put his eye to the vision lens, and twirled the focusing regulator.

At first he saw nothing but a great milky blur. But, as he continued to turn the focusing regulator the milky blur faded away and definite objects, in magnified proportions, took shape before his eyes.

Spread out before him was the northern half of the nation's

capitol. It was as though he were looking at the city in broad daylight. Every building, every street, and even every tree stood out in clear relief.

AS THOUGH to prove to himself that he was not witnessing a miracle, he turned from the vision lens and looked out through the glass windows of the plane. Save for the faint glow in the east he could see nothing but murky darkness. Turning back to the vision piece, he raised one hand and motioned to the right.

"Right rudder, Curly!" he called out. "And nose her down a hair."

Seconds later the entire city of Washington lay spread out before him. Turning the focus regulator for absolute clearness, he stared intently at the squat and square War College building, located about half a mile from the southern bank of the Potomac.

As he looked at the building, which he knew for years had been vacated right down to the last piece of furniture, his pulse quickened and a tingle of expectant excitement surged through him.

"How can they do it?" he muttered aloud. "How in hell can they do it?"

"You tell me, kid, I'm dumb."

Dusty paid no attention to Curly's words and continued to stare at the War College building. Out of the corner of his eye he noted the hands of his wrist watch. They showed exactly one half minute of five.

And then it happened!

A blurred shadow came swooping down from out of nowhere

THE BLURRED SHADOW
STREAKED UP AND WAS GONE

and went streaking across the ground straight for the War College building. So terrific was its speed that at first Dusty was unable to see anything in detail. It was like the shadow cast by a cloud rushing across the face of the sun.

But a split second later it took form and he saw what seemed to be a gigantic shell, pointed at the nose and flanged out horn-shaped at its end. It had no color. Rather it was a mixture of all hues with, perhaps, red predominating.

"There it is—the Red Destroyer!"

Dusty's wild cry echoed back to him as though as it had come from miles away. And almost immediately it was drowned out by Curly's questioning roar.

"What do you mean kid? Do you see anything?"

Dusty made no answer. He didn't hear the voice of his pal. Like a man of stone he sat rigid staring down at the blurred object sweeping across the ground with lightning like rapidity toward the War College building.

And then suddenly the walls of the building crumpled out-wards as though a thousand gallons of liquid Tetalyne had been set off at its foundation. One second the building was intact and the next it was a crumbling heap of ruins, and the shell like object was sweeping up and away to the north.

Dusty gestured frantically with both hands.

"Throttle, Curly!" he bellowed. "Throttle, and bear to the north!"

Before Dusty's last words had raced off his lips Curly had rammed the throttle all the way home and was sending the X-Rayoscope plane thundering across the dawn tinged skies. But though the plane clawed air at maximum revs the shell shaped object virtually leaped up to oblivion and disappeared.

"Speed, Curly!" shouted Dusty. "Give her everything she's got!"

"She's got it!" Curly bellowed back. "But what in hell do you see?"

Dusty didn't answer. Eyes glued to the vision piece, he searched the dawn flooded skies to the north. But in vain. The mysterious object that had crumpled the War College building was gone. On impulse Dusty reached out, snapped on the plane's radio set, spun the wave-length dial and snatched up the transmitter tube.

"Washington H.Q. on seven—four-two!" he shouted. "Captain Ayres calling Washington H.Q. on seven-four-two! Emergency!"

Heart pounding against his ribs he sat waiting breathlessly for a check-back on his call. An eternity passed and then a crisp voice crackled out of the ear phones.

"On your wave-length Captain Ayres! Go ahead!"

Dusty bent close to the transmitter tube.

"Unable to sight object that demolished the War College building!" he snapped out. "It disappeared to the north. Am now flying up the Maine coast. Any orders?"

"Keep contact, Captain Ayres!" crackled the ear phones. "I am switching you over to General Horner."

As the last died away there was suddenly a high keyed hum in the phones. It lasted for perhaps five seconds and then the harsh grating voice of the Black Hawk blasted against Dusty's ear drums.

"Sorry that your little trick did not work, Captain Ayres!" came the taunting words.

Before Dusty could check himself the words raced off his lips.

"Damn your soul!" he roared. "Where the hell are you?"

THE EAR-PHONES made no sound. Presently there was a sharp click and Dusty knew that the Black Hawk had gone off his wave-length. He sat glaring at the instrument panel, a thousand-and-one new and more tantalizing thoughts racing around inside his head.

Putting his eye to the vision piece he again searched the skies ahead. But the picture was the same as before. Nothing but dawn-tinged air, and below, the dimly marked Atlantic coast line.

And then suddenly without warning fingers of steel beat a savage tattoo against the side of the cabin. And a split second later Curly's warning cry rang out.

"Hang on, kid! Darts attacking from right rear! Am going to try and roll out!"

Even as Dusty grabbed for a hold. Curly whipped the plane up and over in a lightning like maneuver. For a moment the fingers of steel ceased drumming against the plane. But as the X-Rayoscope plane leveled off they returned again, and this time with even more savage intensity.

Holding fast, Dusty twisted in the seat and stared up through the glass window in the ceiling of the cabin. As he did, a giant unseen hand smashed through it and showered him with stinging splinters. He ducked and yelled at Curly.

"Down, kid! Spin down!"

Brooks nodded tight-lipped, slammed the stick over and

back and thumped down hard on the right rudder pedal. The plane seemed to virtually groan aloud as it sliced over and down in a power spin. Unable to do anything, Dusty simply sat rigid and hung on, staring down at the faintly lighted ground rushing up toward him. Absently he noted its character and checked with his roller map. What he discovered brought a gasp of surprise to his lips. They were just west of the Bay of Fundy, and over New Brunswick. In other words, over Black territory.

He turned and met Curly's eyes!

"Over Black ground!" he shouted. "Try and work this damn thing south!"

At that instant, as though to mock his shouted words, there came the savage chatter of aerial machine gun fire, and the X-Rayoscope plane seemed to stagger sidewise. Brooks cursed and yanked on the controls, and the plane responded like a water logged vessel in a heavy sea.

"She's not taking it right! A control cable's gone!"

Curly's words were unnecessary as far as Dusty was concerned. The very "feel" of the ship had told him. Lurching up out of his seat he crawled back to his pal.

"Get the chutes out, kid!" he said. "I'll take over."

But Brooks shook his head.

"Get them out yourself. I can make it O.K.!"

The last was punctuated by a new burst of machine gun fire, and one of the cabin windows melted away as though by magic. Again the plane staggered sidewise, and again Curly battled furiously with the controls. After a terrific effort he succeeded in righting the ship. But it was only for an instant. Like a broken bird the plane flopped over on wing and went swinging around like a feather in a whirlpool.

"No use, kid! We're going to smack hard, I guess. And it's too risky to jump. Those damn rats would pick us off like flies."

Dusty nodded and said nothing. Bracing himself as best he could against the cabin wall, he dully watched Curly "fight" the controls. A side glance at the altimeter told him that they were less than eight thousand up. A matter of a couple of minutes now, and it would be all over.

For an instant he was inclined to order Curly out of the seat, and take over himself. But he curbed the urge. They didn't make any pilots better than Curly Brooks. And if Curly couldn't get them down right side up, no one could. Nope, it was just up to him to hang on and take it.

And then on sudden thought, he flung himself forward and snapped on radio contact.

"All American stations!" he roared into the transmitter tube. "Stand by for emergency. Captain Ayres and Lieutenant Brooks about to crash at map position N Twenty-Six—behind the enemy lines. Send help if possible. We will try to hold off ground capture as long as possible."

"Brace, kid, brace! Here we go!"

Dusty dropped the transmitter tube as Curly's shouted alarm rang out. A flash glance through the cabin window showed a glimpse of trees and fields. And then, before he had the chance for a second look the right wings "crabbed" on the top most branches of a tree and he was flung up against the side of the cabin.

What happened in the next few seconds was a thundering conglomeration of sound. A giant fist belted him in the small of his back and knocked him forward. Then a second invisible fist caught him square in the chest, and sent him flat on his back. Head reeling, a great sea of dancing colored light before his eyes, he struggled to get up on his hands and knees. But, it was only to be knocked flat again as the plane plowed down through tree branches and dug its nose into soggy ground. And, the next thing he knew he was lying on his side and staring dully into the rage-twisted features of Curly's face, not a foot away from him.

CHAPTER 7
SOUTHEAST OF GREENLAND

IT TOOK a moment or two for clear memory to come back to him. But when it did, it came with a rush. He put out his hand and touched his pal.

"O.K., kid?" he asked.

Brooks blinked, and then nodded.

"Guess so," he mumbled thickly. "Who in hell put that tree in the way?"

Dusty grinned and got up on his hands and knees. The walls of the cabin had crumpled up like so much tin roofing, and he was forced to crawl to the door. When he reached it he found that the crash had twisted it out of line and it was jammed tight. Though he put his shoulder to it and exerted all of his strength it refused to budge.

They ran toward the
woods as the Darts dove.

"This way out, kid!" Curly called to him. "The window."

He turned from the door, crawled across the cabin floor again, and pulled himself up through the broken window. Curly was already out, and waiting for him. When he reached the ground he straightened up and stared about him.

The plane, which was a complete washout, had crashed in a narrow field, bordered on three sides by woods. If Curly had been able to veer the ship only a shade to the left, they would probably have sat down safely.

He shrugged at the thought and glanced at his pal. Curly was glaring at the broken off top of a tree.

"Damn tree!" he mumbled. "Hell, what a fine pilot I am!"

"Forget it, Curly," said Dusty. "The main thing is that we can still walk. Maybe we would have been as stiff as iced mackerel if I'd had the stick."

Curly grinned.

"Thanks for the cover-up anyway," he said. "But now that we're here—what next?"

The question brought Dusty back to realities. He felt utterly helpless and twice as much of a fool. A perfectly good plane was wrecked, a valuable X-Rayoscope unit destroyed, and two Yank eagles lost far behind the Black Invader lines. And all because of an idea of his!

"Hell!" he grated aloud. "If I—"

The rest was drowned out by the sudden roar of airplane engines, and the savage chatter of machine-gun fire. He shot a snap glance upward, saw the four Darts that were piling down straight for them, and started running toward the woods.

Snappy, Curly!" he shouted back over his shoulder. "The damn bums are trying to finish the job."

His words were a waste of breath. Curly was pounding ground right at his elbow. Together they raced for the protection of the woods as the flame spitting Darts tore down and kicked up dirt with hissing steel.

Perhaps Dusty and Curly were too fast, or perhaps the Blacks were rotten shots, but at any rate the two Yanks reached the woods without a scratch.

As Curly started to pull up, Dusty flung out a hand.

"Don't stop, sap!" he shouted. "Keep going!"

"What the hell for?" panted Brooks, catching up. "They can't pick us off now. Hell, they're even going away."

"Sure," nodded Dusty leaping a fallen log. "But we're in Black territory now, and if you ask me those planes were marking the spot where we were, for their damn ground troops. Distance is our best bet."

Whether Curly agreed or disagreed, he at least made no comment and kept right on running.

Some ten minutes later they plunged out of the heavy underbrush and into a small clearing. They both slowed up instinctively.

"Gosh I'm out of training!" groaned Curly as he sank to the ground. "Or maybe its just age."

Dusty said nothing. He stood looking helpless about, a worried frown on his brow. Then he suddenly turned to Curly and gestured.

"Up, fellow," he said. "This was only a breather. I want to know what's on the other side of those woods."

Brooks cursed and made no move to get up.

"Then go find out!" he snapped. "I'll wait for you here."

"Up, I said! We've got to—"

"Don't move, or I'll shoot!"

THE HARSHLY spoken words came to Dusty's ears like the clanging of fire bells. He started to whip his hand to his holstered gun, but checked himself in time. Ramrod he stood waiting as there came the sound of footsteps behind. Curly, motionless on the ground was staring fixedly up at the morning sky.

"Guess the foot-race is all over!" he breathed softly.

Before Dusty could say anything a tall, hawk-featured Black soldier came around in front of them. He carried an army rifle in his big hands, and the muzzle was trained on them both. His eyes bored into Dusty's for a split second, then slithered down to Curly.

"Get up! Raise your hands—both of you!"

Tight lipped, they obeyed and stood rigid as the Black unholstered their automatics and transferred them to the pockets of his coarse black tunic. Then, a cruel grin on his face, the Black stepped back a pace or two, and nodded slowly, as though he were quite pleased with his thoughts.

"You, I recognize," he said to Dusty. "You are the American flyer, Captain Ayres, yes?"

"So what?" Dusty grunted, his eye on the man's rifle.

"So, it will be very fine for me," the Black replied. "There is still a fine price on your head, captain—dead, or alive. I shall probably get promotion, too."

The man cut his words off short and shoved out his rifle, as Dusty unconsciously swayed forward.

"Be careful, captain!" he barked. "I said dead or alive, you know. It matters little to me which you are!"

Dusty started to speak when from the woods to his left came the sharp crack of a rifle shot. The Black screamed and flung up his arms. His rifle went spinning away, and he went tumbling over on his back. He was probably dead even before he hit the ground.

Like mummies, their hands still raised above their heads, Dusty and Curly stood gaping down at the fallen Black. And then as one man they turned to stare at a second Black soldier who was running out of the woods. Even when he skidded to a halt in front of them, they still gaped.

"The make-up must be good, if you lads don't know me!"

"My God, you!" cried Dusty.

"Jack Horner!" Curly chimed in in almost the same breath. "Well, I'll be a—"

"Sure," grinned Agent 10. "Aren't you going to thank me?"

Dusty lowered his hands, gripped the shoulders of the fierce looking figure in front of him and squeezed hard.

"Thank you?" he echoed. "Fellow, I could almost kiss you. But how—"

He stopped short, and glanced around.

"Hadn't we better get going?" he asked. "Maybe some of the others are around."

The Black screamed and
flung up his hands.

"An idea," nodded Agent 10. "No sense taking chances, anyway. Here, follow me."

With a nod he turned and started across the clearing. Pausing long enough to stoop down and retrieve their guns from the dead Black's pocket, Dusty and Curly followed. A thousand and one questions burned on Dusty's lips, but he didn't speak to them. Agent 10 didn't give him the chance to.

Walking rapidly, the Intelligence man lead them into the woods and along a faint, almost indistinguishable foot path.

As Dusty stared at the man's back he had the feeling that Jack Horner had been in these woods many times before. He didn't hesitate in his pace once. Just kept right on going at a rapid gate, turning now right, and now left. But, eventually he stopped in front of a large and thick clump of underbrush.

Turning, he grinned at them and gestured.

"How's this for apples?" he said. "Guess we can be bright, too, when we want to. Enter and make yourself at home."

As he spoke young Horner reached out and grasped hold of the nearest bush. To Dusty's utter amazement the bush swung to one side to reveal the door of a tiny wooden hut, completely hidden in the brush. He gaped at Agent 10.

"Well—what the hell's this?" he gasped.

"Go through the door and find out," grinned Agent 10.

Dusty hesitated, then brushed past him and pulled open the door. The first thing he saw as he stepped inside was a mass of radio and teletype equipment. He stopped dead and stared at it dumbfounded. Curly pushed him into the room and gasped aloud.

"My God! Am I seeing things?"

"You're seeing plenty!" chuckled Agent 10 as he came in and closed the door. "Park on the floor. It's the best I can offer."

Words failing them, Dusty and Curly sat down on the floor. Agent 10 stepped over their legs and squatted down in front of a radio panel. He hooked earphones over his head, but kept one ear uncovered.

"Expecting something to come through," he said, as they stared at him.

"For the love of Pete!" Dusty broke out. "How long has this place been here?"

"About a week," answered Jack Horner. "But tell me your story. I picked some of your messages out of the air. Lucky for you I got that S.O.S. crash message. And a lucky break for us all that you crashed near where I've been hanging out."

Dusty leaned forward.

"And you weren't at H-Six yesterday afternoon?" he asked. "Wasn't it you that took that crack at Fire-Eyes—shot him?"

It was Agent 10's turn to look dumbfounded.

"Shot Fire-Eyes?" he echoed. "Good God, no! I haven't seen him for days. But wait, let's start at the beginning. You tell your story, and then I'll tell mine."

KEEPING IT as brief as possible, yet not leaving out any of the important details, Dusty told him of all that had happened. Agent 10 didn't interrupt once. He sat listening in frowning silence.

"And I guess that I've just been wasting government property," Dusty finished up bitterly. "We're just as much in the dark as ever."

"No, I wouldn't say that," grunted Agent 10. "You've at least made contact with me. And that's something I've been hoping for, for the last twenty-four hours. You see, I've been trying to get through to you, but couldn't. The Blacks know that I'm around somewhere, and that I've been trying to contact Washington H.Q. ever since I got that one message through to my father. And so they've static-jammed the entire front line area."

The Intelligence man paused long enough to jerk a thumb at the radio panel.

"I can sit here and listen to their jabber," he said. "But I can't get a damn thing out myself. Don't dare try just now, anyway. Can't risk their tracking it down with a directional finder. But, you heard a shot, eh? Poor old Bob! He would stick, when I warned him that it was too risky."

"Meaning just what?" asked Curly.

"Bob was one of the lads working with me," explained Agent 10. "Together we set up that Telerad station at H-Six. But, damn them, the Blacks caught on. Bob and I cleared out just in time to save our skins. The Blacks must have listened in as I sent that last message through. Bob and I split. Hell, I had no idea that he'd go back. He had nothing to send through, anyway. At least I don't think he did. Poor devil, I wonder if he got away again.

"I'm wondering if he got Fire-Eyes," spoke up Dusty.

Agent 10 shook his head vigorously.

"Not a chance," he said. "I thought that Bob knew. Most

everyone else does. You see, Fire-Eyes' uniform and mask are made of bullet proof mesh. There are a few in his own gang who would like to take a shot at him, if they dared. So, he keeps himself protected, just in case."

"About my story, Jack," said Dusty impatiently. "How does it check up with what you know? Or don't you know anything? What is this damn thing? And—"

He stopped short as Agent 10 suddenly gestured for silence, and slipped the other phone over his ear. He listened intently for several seconds, then grimaced and removed the phone.

"Just troop orders," he grunted. "Been coming through all day. They're strengthening the line from one end to the other. Yeah, getting ready for that damn offensive."

"Offensive?" echoed Curly excitedly. "By God, Dusty, I bet you're right! That armistice thing is a stall!"

"Of course it is!" nodded Agent 10. "Now listen, fellows— here's what I know of the picture. The Blacks have a new weapon of war. It's something that can strike from the air—a new kind of ship, or something. I had hoped to get details, but I failed. But, I did learn this much. Only one has been completed. It was for experimental purposes. And—whatever it is, its being based at the old Great Circle sea-drome about seven hundred miles southeast of Cape Farewell, Greenland.

"From what I can learn, no real attack on America will be made until more of these weapons are completed. I think they're made some place in Europe—I don't know for sure. But as you guessed, Dusty, the Blacks are playing for time—time in which to get this new secret weapon set to give us a dozen different kinds of hell."

"The old Great Circle seadrome, eh?" mused Dusty. "Say, our Atlantic fleet would like to hear about that! Let's get through to them and give the warning. Then they can steam up and blast the place to bits."

AGENT 10 pursed his lips and looked dubious.

"I doubt it," he said slowly. "First, there's no way for us to get word through—we're static-jammed on all messages going south. Secondly, even if we did get word through, the Blacks would pick it up and undoubtedly change their base before the fleet could steam north.

"Thirdly, the seadrome is protected by their own planes and battleship squadrons. They've been using it for a midway depot for supplies from Europe ever since the outbreak of the war. And fourthly, if the damn thing picked off the *Texas, Utah* and *Vermont* so easily—it could probably do the same to the ships of the Atlantic fleet."

"Then let's get them by air!" cried Dusty, exasperatedly. "Let's bomb the hell out of the place. Our lads could sink that seadrome in a ten minute raid!"

Again Agent 10 looked dubious.

"I still say no, for the same reasons," he grunted.

"But hell, kid," insisted Dusty, "what are we going to do, sit here and twiddle our thumbs while those devils get away with murder? My God, if you'd seen that Federal Building fold up, you'd know exactly how I feel."

"I do know," nodded the Intelligence man. "But—hold it!"

Young Horner had slipped the phone back on his ear and was listening intently, a heavy frown creasing his brows, and a wild light of excitement blazing up in his eyes. It was all Dusty could do to sit still and wait. He wanted to grab one of the phones and listen himself. But he realized that that would be useless. He didn't know the Blacks' high speed secret code. So clamping savagely down on his nerves he sat rigid, eyes fixed on Agent 10's face.

Though it was only a matter of a couple of minutes it seemed a life-time to Dusty before Agent 10 snapped down a switch and removed the ear-phones. He turned to them quickly.

"That's one for our side, anyway!" he breathed fiercely. "I've been hoping against hope that I would pick up that message!"

Dusty cursed softly.

"What message?" he asked. "For the love of mike spill it, will you?"

Young Horner took a deep breath and hesitated as though choosing his words.

"Did you know" he said looking at Dusty, "that the Black Hawk and his brood vacated their drome about a week ago?"

"Yes, I did. Go ahead."

"Well I have just found out where they are based," said young Horner. "What I listened to just now was a Black High Command order for all planes of Black Unit No. 10 to concentrate at Cape Farewell drome for auxiliary maneuvers."

"And that means?" from Dusty.

"It means just what I've been expecting," replied Agent 10.

"That the Hawk's Unit is going to work with that damn thing they are keeping at the Great Circle drome."

Dusty shrugged and made an impetuous gesture with his hands.

"Well that's something I suppose," he said gloomily. "But what—say wait a minute, just where are we?"

"About fourteen miles due north of Fredericton," answered Agent 10. "Why?"

Dusty grinned and bunched his fist.

"Just this. Listen, unless I'm wrong, the Black's have a replacement depot near here haven't they?"

"They have one," said Agent 10. "It's about six miles due east of us."

Dusty glanced at Curly Brooks.

"Are you game to try it, kid?" he asked.

Curly nodded.

"Sure," he said. "When do we start?"

"Wait a minute!" Agent 10 broke in. "What do you mean? Try what?"

"A crazy idea," said Dusty. "Now listen, according to your own words, the place that we are interested in is the Great Circle seadrome, off the Greenland coast. It's guarded both by air and sea, and so it wouldn't be much help even if we did get word through to our boys. And, so that leaves just one thing for us to do—take a crack at it ourselves. Now here's the plan. It isn't much, but good enough for a starter. You show us the way to this replacement depot and Curly and I will try to swipe a ship. From there on we'll trust to luck."

Agent 10 stared fixedly at the opposite wall.

"It is a crazy idea," he said softly. "But just what do you think you can do?"

Dusty shrugged.

"Sneak through the Black blockade, and get aboard that seadrome," he said. "If we have half the luck that we had at Chihuahua it will be fair enough."

"And then some!" put in Curly.

There followed a long moment of silence. It was young Horner who finally broke it.

"We're up against it," he said bitterly. "And as I have not got any ideas of my own, I'm forced to agree with yours. However, here is one thing upon which I insist. We're going to make it a party of three. Safety in numbers, you know."

Dusty grinned.

"I was expecting that," he said. "And it's O.K. with us, eh, Curly?"

"Suits me," nodded Brooks. "But how about getting started?"

"No time like the present," said young Horner getting to his feet. "But wait a minute."

He put a hand into the side pocket of his coarse black uniform, pulled out a small flask and help it up.

"Just a spot for luck," he grinned. "And if you ask me we're going to need plenty of it."

CHAPTER 8
FAKE ORDERS

TWO HOURS later the three of them were crouching in the thick underbrush that dotted the crest of a small hill over-looking the Black replacement drome northeast of Fredericton. Under Agent 10's skillful guidance, the six mile trip through the very heart of Black occupied territory had been made without any unusual incident.

Though both Dusty and Curly knew full well of young Horner's qualities and capabilities they could not help but marvel at the sixth sense he seemed to possess. Without him they would have stumbled into trouble in the form of Black patrols a dozen different times. But the Intelligence man always spotted them in the nick of time and quickly detoured out of danger.

But now, as Dusty gazed fixedly down at the small field with it's row of four hangars bordering the near side and the assortment of all types of planes lined up in front, he realized with a sinking feeling that the job hadn't even been started.

The field was practically alive with Black mechanics and pilots. For him or Curly to show their faces would bring a hundred Blacks with guns on a dead run.

As though Curly had read his thoughts, the lean pilot turned to Dusty and shook his head.

"Not so good," he grunted.

"No," said Dusty. Then added grimly, "But we've got to make it good. Any ideas?"

As Curly spoke he pointed a finger at the right end of the line of planes.

"See that amphibian?" he said. "The second in from the right? I'd say that that is our best bet. They shut off the engine a couple of minutes ago, so she'll be hot. And there's only a couple of the bums hanging around her. What do you think?"

Dusty nodded.

"I think you're right," he said. "We've got to take a chance and rush them anyway. We can't hang around here all day. I suggest that we work to the right and come down through that narrow strip of woods. That will bring us out about forty yards from the ship. Do you check with me, Jack?"

Agent 10 who had been listening, nodded shortly.

"I do," he said. "But listen to me, a second. If the three of us rush the plane at the same time we're bound to be spotted by someone, and all hell will break loose. Now why not do it this way? We'll all go down to that strip of woods, and then I'll saunter over to the plane and try to draw those Black mechanics away.

"Watch my right hand. When you see me scratch my face, go hell-for-leather for the plane. I'll try and have the cabin door already open. The instant you're inside, I'll clout those two birds and make a dive for it. The only thing is, what if they come up after us in those pursuits? That amphib can't run away from them."

"No, it can't," said Dusty. "But Nature is going to give us the break that we need. See that cloud bank off to the left? You leave it to me to lose them in it. Well, here goes. Come on!"

KEEPING WELL down in the underbrush the three Yanks crawled on their hands and knees across the brow of the hill and down its western slope to the narrow strip of scraggly woods. But as they reached it and straightened up, Curly Brooks suddenly let out a low cry, spun around and virtually hurled his body through the air. So fast had been his movements that before Dusty and Agent 10 realized what was taking place, it was all over. At Curly's feet lay the crumpled figure of a burly Black guard. His rifle was still clutched in his hands, and the forefinger curled about the trigger. But he would not fire that gun for many hours to come.

The darkening bruise on his right temple was silent evidence that Curly's aim with the butt of his automatic had been perfect.

"My gosh, kid!" gasped Dusty. "I didn't even see him!"

"Me either!" exclaimed Agent 10. "But for you we would have been in one hell of a fix."

"Forget it," grunted Curly. "It's about time I added something to the party. Let's go."

On the alert more than ever, they made their way silently through the narrow strip of woods and finally came to a crouching stop behind a large clump of bushes.

A little over forty yards in front of them was the near end of the line of planes. Two Black mechanics lounged against the wing of the first plane which was a high speed monoplane bomber.

There was no one near the amphibian. Save for the two mechanics, the nearest Black was over a hundred yards away.

Dusty turned to Agent 10, reached out and gripped his hand.

"O.K. kid," he said softly. "Luck! Will be seeing you shortly."

With a grin and a nod for them both, young Horner straightened up, slung his rifle carelessly in the crook of his arm, and walked slowly away to the right. Dusty and Curly watched him out of sight in the underbrush and then turned their eyes back to the monoplane bomber.

Seconds dragged by and became a minute—two minutes—three, and then they saw the figure of Agent 10 walking leisurely over toward the Black mechanics. They turned and stared at him as he approached. One of them said something and Agent 10 answered, but neither Dusty nor Curly heard what it was.

Bodies crouched rigid, hands gripping their guns for instant use, they watched with bated breath as young Horner offered cigarettes to the Blacks and continued to talk with them.

"God, that's what I call guts, even though he is used to it!"

Dusty made no comment to Curly's exclamation. Words were useless now. Action was in the offing. So he continued to silently watch the drama taking place before him and steeled himself for instant movement.

Agent 10 was faking curiosity in the planes and slowly drawing the two Black mechanics farther and farther away from the amphibian. When they were perhaps thirty yards on the far side, they paused and appeared to start a friendly argument. Dusty could see the two Blacks gesticulating with their hands, and Agent 10 first nodding and then shaking his head.

Without turning his head, Dusty reached out and touched Curly on the shoulder.

"Set, kid!" he breathed. "Any second now!"

As a matter of fact it happened in less than three seconds. Young Horner's right hand came up and scratched his face.

For Dusty and Curly, sight and action were one. Springing to their feet they dove out of the clump of bushes and went racing toward the line of planes. They reached the monoplane bomber in the matter of split seconds, ducked under its wing and fuselage and came up beside the amphibian.

Without checking their speed they ducked under it and came up on the door side. A quick outward thrust of his hand and a twist, and Dusty had the door open.

As he scrambled inside, and virtually flung himself into the pilot's seat, he heard a wild cry behind him. A moment later there was the crash of a rifle, and a voice cried out in mortal pain. He didn't dare risk a look back. He thumped down on the electric starter, and opened the throttle. The engine caught on the first rev, and the plane tugged at his wheel brakes.

"Let her go!" came Curly's roar. "Jack can make it. Let her go!"

SNAPPING OFF the wheel brakes, Dusty sent the ship rolling out onto the field. Twisting in the seat he glanced back. Through the open door he could see Agent 10, his rifle gone, racing furiously for the plane. Curly was hanging out of the open door and waving him on.

Hardly realizing what he was doing, Dusty hauled back the throttle and tapped the wheel brakes. His instinctive action undoubtedly saved young Horner's life. At the speed the plane

Curly grabbed Horner's arm and pulled him into the cabin.

had been traveling, the Intelligence man couldn't possibly have made it.

As it happened, he only made it by a hair, and Curly Brooks' strong right arm. The lean pilot reached out, grabbed hold of Horner's arm and practically threw him over his shoulder into the cabin of the cockpit. Then he ducked back in himself and slammed the door.

"Let her out, Dusty! For God's sake, let her out!"

As Curly shouted the order, rifles cracked outside and steel bullets smacked against the cabin walls and metal hull of the amphibian.

A few seconds later, as Dusty got the tail up and went thundering across the field, ground-pit machine guns opened fire and a criss-cross hail of death showered the plane.

Hunching forward over the Dep control, Dusty clenched his teeth and savagely cursed the plane on to greater speed. Out the corner of his eye he could see Black pilots racing for the line of ships. A prop on one of them was already turning over. He cursed, and smashed his free fist against the throttle.

"Move, damn you!" he shouted wildly. "Get going!"

As though the plane were something alive and had actually heard his words, its wheels cleared a split second later and it went zooming up into a cloud-bank filled sky.

Cranking the wheels up into the hull to gain every iota of speed possible, Dusty held the nose up and swung around toward the billowy cloud bank to the east. Five minutes flying, and they'd make it.

He glanced back down at the field and groaned. Five minutes? He'd have to make it in less than that. Two sleek pursuit planes were streaking across the field, He switched his eyes back to the front, and stared at the twin guns faired into the nose of the amphibian hull.

"Curly—Jack!" he shouted.

A hand touched his shoulder, and two voices spoke as one. "Yeah? What?"

He didn't bother to turn and look at them.

"Get set, the best you can," he said grimly. "I was wrong. We haven't a hope in hell of making that cloud bank. Two of them are already coming up after us. The only way out is a scrap!"

"Go to it, kid," came Curly's even voice. "Don't bother about us. We'll manage to hang on some how."

Dusty nodded appreciation of their trust in him, swung the plane over and around on wing tip. The Blacks were still a couple of thousand feet below him. But they were coming up fast. To continue straight for the cloud bank, and wait for them to attack, would be plain suicide.

There was only one thing to do. Fake an escape to the south, keep an eye on the Blacks, and then suddenly slap down on the first one to come within range.

Eyes hard, hands on the Dep wheel rock-steady, he sent the amphibian racing southward. The pursing Blacks swallowed the fake maneuver hook, line and sinker. In an almost vertical climb they came thundering upward.

Nearer and nearer they came, and in the matter of seconds Dusty could actually see the cruel featured Black crouched under the glass cowling of the nearest plane. He counted four more seconds in his brain, then swung the Dep wheel with all his might, and practically jumped on the right rudder pedal.

The amphibian groaned and bucked, and for the space of a split second it slid sluggishly off to the side. And then with a snapping twist it whipped over and down. As it did, Dusty jerked both thumbs up to the trigger trips and jabbed them forward. The twin guns in the nose of the hull spat jetting flame and a withering blast of steel cut down across the sky at the nearest Black ship.

Had Dusty made any other maneuver, the Black pilot would probably have been ready. But so utterly crazy was the one that he did make, that the Black went completely haywire for the instant and did the wrong thing.

He leveled off the top of his climb and tried to bank around, instead of slicing over-wing to Dusty. But he didn't and the Yank eagle leaped upon him like a streak of light.

Steel bullets smashed his glass cowling to splinters and whipped down into his skull and body. Two short bursts, and that was all that was needed. The Black pilot slumped over against the side of the cockpit. The plane went curving around in a great circle and then as its motion threw the lifeless Black forward onto the stick it went racing earthward, its throttle wide open.

"One! Atta kid!"

DUSTY HARDLY heard Curly's shouted cry. He was too occupied trying to draw the second Black pursuit ship into a similar trap. But, after seeing what had happened to his comrade, the second Black wasn't having any more of that stuff. Rolling and zooming, he darted in and around the slower ship; peppering it with short, tantalizing bursts, but not leaving himself open for more than a split second at a time.

Try as he might, Dusty could not keep pace with the sleek ship. He fired whenever he got the chance, but each time it was simply a waste of good ammunition. One thing, however, was in his favor. The Black, not wanting to risk his neck too much, was making no effort to drive Dusty in any one particular direction. He seemed content to dart in, pepper a few shots, and then dart out into the clear again.

Taking advantage of that fact, Dusty made no real attacking

attempt. Instead he concentrated on working the amphibian eastward toward the cloud bank. It was less than three miles away when the Black pilot evidently realized what was taking place.

Abandoning his safety-first tactics, he half-rolled off the top of a loop and came slicing down with guns blazing. The sudden maneuver caught Dusty off guard for a second and before he could skid the amphibian outward and down, the Black had smashed a savage blast through the window in the top of the cabin and buried it in the instrument board.

"Don't let him get you kid!" roared Curly. "Give him hell. He's a cinch!"

But Dusty wasn't even listening. Cursing himself for being asleep, he zoomed the amphibian up and over on to its back, reached out and cut the throttle and let the ship fall off into a slow spin. Curly shouted again, as he clutched frantically for a more secure hold. But this time his shout was one of alarm.

"My God, Dusty! Are you crazy? He'll pick us up like apples!"

"You just hang on, I'm doing this!" he bellowed angrily, and hand-heeled the throttle wide open.

As he did, he slammed the Dep wheel over to the opposite corner held it there for a fraction of a second, then hauled it back into his stomach and thumped down on the left rudder. The plane seemed to actually moan in protest and its nose jerked up and it went wing-screaming heavenward. Dusty held it steady for perhaps three hundred feet, then whipped it over on right wing and sent it slicing diagonally down across the sky. Out the corner he saw the Black pilot striving desperately to follow through the maneuver. He slid his thumbs to the trigger-trips and laughed harshly.

"Too bad, bum!" He shouted. "But I'm in a hurry!"

As he spoke the last, he jabbed the trigger-trips forward and the twin guns in the nose of the hull yammered out a hymn of certain death. And certain death it was.

The Black was caught flat-footed. He probably died before he even realized what had hit him. One second he was a human being alive and flying through the air. And the next, he was a corpse hurtling earthward, the center of an alarming cloud of flame and smoke.

Dusty didn't even give the plane a second look. The instant he saw the flames belch out, he pulled the amphibian out of its thundering angle dive, and sent it rocketing up into the misty protection of the billowy cloud bank. Easing back the throttle a bit, he turned in the seat and grinned at Curly and Agent 10.

"What were you boys trying to tell me?" he chuckled.

Agent 10 shook his head, relaxed his hold on the side of the cabin, and swallowed hard. Curly Brooks blinked and muttered a curse.

"Go ahead, kid, and ride me!" he grunted. "I sure deserve it. My God, if that last one wasn't one for the book, then I sure give up!"

"I'll be glad to teach it to you sometime when I have time." Dusty grinned.

AND THEN his eyes swept the bullet-shattered instrument board, and his face became grave. Reaching out his free hand he absently fingered the electromagnetic compass that had been hopelessly riddled with singing steel. His hand still on the compass he turned again to his pals.

"I guess we'd better hang up here for a while," he said. "I didn't have a chance to look, but maybe some of those other babies started up after us, when they saw their other boy friends go down. With this damn compass gone, we'll have to make a double check with the roller-map and take our bearings from what we find out. Is that oke with you?"

Curly hadn't quite completely recovered from Dusty's display of perfect aerial scrapping. He nodded his head almost automatically.

"Sure, anything you say, kid," he mumbled.

Agent 10, however, shook his head and leaned toward Dusty.

"Why waste the time?" he asked. "I've got an idea and I think it will work. Here, move over, and let me get at the radio."

Wondering what was on young Horner's mind, Dusty shifted over on the seat and let him squeeze in beside him. Reaching out both hands, the Intelligence man snapped on power contact with one hand, slipped the earphones over his head with the other, spun the wave-length dial and put his lips to the transmitter tube.

Seconds later, he was jabbering excitedly into it—jabbering out countless inarticulate sounds in the language of the Black Invaders. He kept it up for perhaps three minutes, paused to listen to a replying jabber in the ear phones, then spoke for another minute or two.

"There, that's that," he said snapping off the radio and grinning at Dusty, "You can fly east out of this cloud bank and get your bearings anytime you want."

Dusty stared at him, brows furrowed.

"All right I'll bite," he grunted. "What the hell did you do?"

"Oh, nothing much," replied Agent 10. "I simply sent out an S.O.S. emergency call stating that I had picked up this plane one hundred miles west of here, and wanted help in giving chase and forcing it down. The reply I got was that every available plane would concentrate on that area immediately."

Dusty let out a wild whoop and rammed the throttle wide open.

"Am I glad you came along!" he yelled. "Now for the last lap, and some more of that luck!"

CHAPTER 9
THE SEADROME

A S AGENT 10 climbed out of the seat, Dusty put the controls on the robot climbing regulator and stood up. Peeling off his tunic, he nodded at the other two.

"Shed, you chaps," he ordered. "I'm going up for altitude, so we'll have to stop up that busted window. I think that our three tunics will be enough."

"If they're not we won't have to worry about it long!" grunted Curly, as he and Agent 10 complied with Dusty's request. "Now if you hadn't let that—"

"Yeah, I know!" Dusty cut him off. "But you mustn't expect

everything! Here you do the job. We're reaching ceiling on this cloud bank. It's not so thick as I thought it was."

Dropping back into the seat, Dusty snapped off robot control and leveled off just as the top wing of the amphibian cut up through the fleecy crest of the cloud bank, and into clear sun-flooded air.

At first, he could see nothing but rolling waves of cloud stretching off to the four horizons. After a minute or two of checking his position in relation to the shadow that his plane cast upon the clouds, he banked to the right and flew steadily eastward, his eyes searching for a hole in the cloud.

He didn't find it for another fifteen minutes. By that time Curly and Agent 10 had stuffed up the broken window with their tunics, and were standing behind his seat helping him to find a hole that exposed enough of the terrain below for checking with the roller-map.

As a matter of fact, it was Curly who actually sighted the hole first. He leaned over, touched Dusty's shoulder, and pointed off to the right almost at the same instant that Dusty saw it himself.

Three minutes later, they were circling directly over the open space, and staring down intently at the ground markings far below. On the fifth time around, Dusty nodded.

"I've got it!" he said. "That's Moncton down there. If we hold this dead on course, we'll pass over the tips of Prince Edward and Breton Islands and hit Harbor Grace, New Foundland, right on the nose."

Curly bent over his shoulder and squinted hard at the roller-map.

"Yup, that's right!" he grunted. "Stick her on robot control, just in case our reckoning goes hay-wire."

"Robot control, my eye!" snorted Dusty, glancing at his watch. "I'm going to smoke this baby along at full revs. It's damn near three o'clock now, and if you ask me, even if our luck holds out and we make the damn sea drome, we won't possibly make it before dark."

"I've been thinking about that," spoke up Agent 10. "And frankly it's not going to make me mad. I'd much rather sneak into it in the dark than risk landing in broad daylight. You see it's a cinch that our escape is going to be rebroadcast. And though maybe you didn't notice it, the markings on the tail of this ship are a mile high and twice as wide."

"Got me again!" grinned Dusty. "That gives me an idea. You slide in along side of me, and keep your ear clamped to those phones, while I do the flying. You never can tell what you might pick up. Curly! You stick your nose up against that cabin window there, and check with the roller-map every time you get a chance."

FOR THE next two hours, not a single word was spoken in the cabin, save when Dusty and Curly consulted each other as to the plane's approximate position.

They had long since dropped land at Harbor Grace, and were now thundering out over the rolling waters of the Atlantic. The sun, the only definite object from which they could take their direction bearings, was sliding down over the western rim of the world.

In another hour, darkness would set in, and from that time on their fate would largely depend upon Dusty's inborn navigation skill, and a whole lot of luck.

Though none of them mentioned it to the others, all three realized more and more the seriousness of the reckless and spur of the moment risk they were taking.

What they would meet at the end of their journey only the gods know. But one thing was certain, no matter what they did meet, death would be lurking near.

Perhaps they were crazy fools for ever having even thought of attempting such a wild and insane adventure. And then again maybe not. However, yes or no, they were on their way, and beyond that ever darkening eastern horizon fate awaited them.

Suddenly, Agent 10, who had been sitting like a statue of stone, radio phones clamped tightly over his ears, jerked up straight in the seat and shot out a hand to the reception volume control dial.

As he did, Dusty half turned and stared eagerly at the expression on the Intelligence man's face. At first, it was one of startled surprise. Then it slowly changed to uneasy consternation. And finally to a look of grim worry.

Before he could stop himself, Dusty reached out and grabbed young Horner's arm.

"What is it, kid!" he whispered hoarsely. "What the hell is up?"

Agent 10 shook off his hand and motioned vigorously for

silence. Tight-lipped and narrow-eyed, both Curly and Dusty waited for their friend to speak.

Though it seemed like five years, it was only a matter of five minutes before young Horner removed one of the phones from his ears and looked at them wide-eyed.

Dusty cursed as the man continued to hesitate.

"Damn it, Horner!" he snapped. "What the devil is it?"

"We're sunk!" came the thick answer. "We might just as well turn back while we have a chance."

"Turn back?" yelped Curly Brooks. "Why what the—?"

The look on young Horner's face stopped him short. It was as though the man had suddenly received the news of the complete defeat of the United States by the Black Invaders. Impulsively, Dusty reached out his hand and laid it on his friend's shoulder.

"Take it easy," he said quietly. "Chin up. Now give it to us straight."

Young Horner's lips moved, but no words came out. And eventually when they did, they sounded as though they had come from the bottom of his boots.

"That was high speed code," he began, "from the H.Q. of the Black high command. They know that we're headed for the Great Circle seadrome!"

"What? Impossible!"

Dusty and Curly shouted the words in the same breath.

Agent 10 nodded his head.

"They do know?" he said. "Or at least their guess is strong enough to make them send out the warning. In another half hour the air will be black with their ships. I even heard a check-back from the Hawk's new concentration drome at Cape Fare-well. They're taking off immediately. Better head south, Dusty. We couldn't make it now in a hundred thousand years!"

Dusty said nothing. He sat staring at the radio panel as his whole inside seemed to fold up. Good God, was then nothing that those damn rats didn't find out?

"Listen, Jack," he said. "Are you sure you got the message right? How in the world could they have found out?"

Agent 10 shrugged.

"I got the message correctly," he said. "And as for how they found out—well I can make a guess, a good one. We've been saps, and me the biggest one of all for not thinking of it."

"What do you mean?"

"They've been tracing our course," replied young Horner. "Rather, they probably traced it up as far as Harbor Grace—with ground detectors. Don't you see, once they got wise to my fake order, they contacted ground detector unit over the entire area. It was a cinch for them to pick up this engine. We would be the only plane in the area. All the other had gone racing west-ward. Once they got our course they simply had to add two and two and get the right answer."

"Right answer?" echoed Curly. "I don't get you."

"That we were headed for the Great Circle seadrome," Agent 10 told him. "Look—the Hawk knows that you are trying to find out about the Red Destroyer. He knows that you came up north. And he also must know that you were shot down. Those ships that got you were his ships. A plane is stolen, and it flies

115

a course straight for Harbor Grace, and then out to sea. Hell, do you think that guy is deaf, dumb and blind?"

Curly grimaced.

"My error," he grunted, and looked at Dusty. "Well, kid, what's the old brain thinking? It's a hell of a long way back, if you ask me."

Dusty met his eye, saw the glint in it, and grinned.

"I'm thinking that, too," he said. "The short-cut is to that damn seadrome."

"Man, you're crazy!" exclaimed Horner. "Why, my God, do you think we can defeat the whole damn Black Air Force in this lumbering crate?"

"Who said anything about scrapping the whole Black air force?" Dusty cut him off. "I'll be tickled pink if we don't see any of them."

"But you will, you will!" insisted Agent 10. "You mark my word, in half an hour-"

"We'll be a whole lot of miles from here!" Dusty finished. "You want me to turn south? O.K., we will. And then we'll slide up and around and come in on our friends from the east. How'll that be?"

The other shrugged and gestured hopelessly.

"Go ahead, then," he grunted. "I can't get off and walk away."

"And wouldn't if you could, you old hell-bender!" laughed Dusty, poking him in the ribs. "Just keep that set working, and watch papa!"

AS AGENT 10 turned back to the radio, Dusty glanced at Curly, winked, and swung the ship south. The air was almost entirely bathed in shadows now and the western horizon but a tiny yellow glow. He looked at it and pressed his lips together in a thin, grim line. When that light died he'd be up against the stiffest navigating job of his entire flying career.

True, the robot control would hold him on a dead ahead course, and by checking with its recording dial he could keep track of wind drift, and make allowances. But if he only had the electro-magnetic compass he could set an exact course for any point in the ocean, and make it right on the nose. Without it, it was a case of flying blind and "feeling" his way to the ship.

He shrugged, and stared straight ahead. Presently, he jumped a foot as Curly's hand clamped down on his shoulder.

"What the—"

"Look kid," said Brooks. "Way back there on our left rear quarter. Do you see what I see?"

Dusty twisted in the seat, leaned over toward the cabin window and stared back. All he saw were blurred puffs of cloud in twilight darkening sky. And then, suddenly, he saw them—a great swarm of black wings tearing westward in double line formation.

He thought that they were a mixture of bi-planes and monoplanes, but he couldn't say for sure. The distance was too great. He nodded grimly to himself, started to bank east, then on second thought kept right on heading south.

"Keep your tail to them, dummy!" he growled to himself. "Want them to come over and smack you down?"

"Right!" came Curly's voice. "I was all ready to grab the

controls myself. This is a break—they're going right past our stern. Hold her as she goes for another half hour, anyway, kid."

And at the end of that half hour they were roaring through a great, limitless void of inky darkness. Not daring to snap on any of the lights, not even the instrument cowl lamp, Dusty held the ship on even keel by instinct.

"Curly," he said to his pal crouched beside him. "Take a good look for lights, in the air and on the water. I'm going to turn east."

As Curly pressed his face against the window, Dusty eased the plane around in a ninety degree turn and flattened out. And it was then that he saw them—a faint tiny string of lights far down on the water below. Curly saw them at the same instant and gripped his arm.

"Ships, Dusty! And they're too far north to be Yank boats. They must be Blacks—maybe part of the Great Circle blockade."

"Maybe," grunted Dusty, peering down at the lights through narrowed eyes. "I only hope to God they haven't got engine detectors aboard. I don't want any of their wings coming up for a look-see."

As he finished, Agent 10 suddenly broke into rapid Black Invader jabber. Though Dusty couldn't see him very clearly, he knew that the Intelligence man was speaking into the transmitter tube. His voice rose angrily, faded down, only to go up again. It was clear that Jack Horner was acting the perfect Black Invader officer and tearing into some one of lesser rank.

Eventually the man ceased speaking, and Dusty felt him lean toward him.

"Got something that time, blast them!" came the savage voice in the darkness. "A flotilla of Black destroyers below us, picked up our engine. Their operator wanted to know where we were heading and why. I told him the truth, and asked for our exact position. Dusty, we're two hundred and ten miles southeast of the Great Circle seadrome!"

Dusty whistled aloud.

"My God!" he exclaimed. "We must have been almost on top of it when we turned. Thanks, kid. Keep up the good work. Risk another check with some ship in, say, half an hour. That is, if you think you can get away with it."

"Oke," grunted Agent 10 and turned back to his set.

"Spill it!" snapped Dusty, as he heard Curly's soft chuckle in his ear. "Must I be right all the time?"

"And papa was heading for Spain!" his pal cracked back. "That's the first time I was ever really glad to sight Black ships."

"Aw, go fly a kite!" snarled Dusty, and hunched forward over the Dep wheel.

BUT INWARDLY he was sighing with great relief. Had not Agent 10 checked their position with the Black flotilla below, they would eventually have become hopelessly lost over the rolling Atlantic. He must have turned more southeast than east when he made that turn, and without realizing it they were practically flying away from the location of the seadrome.

With a muttered curse he gripped the dep wheel tightly and swung the plane into a slow bank to the left. Halfway around he checked it and flattened out.

"All right, bright eyes!" he flung over his shoulder at Curly.

119

'Stay awake. If they're still using that old landing beacon on the Great Circle, we should be able to pick it up pretty soon. Help me look for it."

"Sure," came Brooks' voice. "And sorry about the ribbing, kid. I wouldn't have done half as well myself. But listen, we haven't done much thinking about what's next on the program. I mean, after we get to the place. Now that they know about this ship we can't possibly land on the seadrome itself. What do you plan to do—glide in with a dead engine close by and swim the rest of the way?"

Dusty didn't answer at once. He was thinking hard. Curly was dead right—they hadn't thought anything about the landing. Hell, was it going to be a waste of time after all? Maybe Agent 10 had the right idea, and they should skip while the skipping was good.

It wasn't fear of death that had made Jack Horner insist that they turn back. He didn't know that kind of fear. It had been the fear of a sane and level-headed man who did not wish to see human lives tossed away when no possible goal could be attained.

"What's your answer, kid?" repeated Curly when Dusty didn't speak. "How do you figure to go down?"

"Your way, I guess," mumbled Dusty. "Your—"

He stopped short and pointed ahead at a thin revolving beam of light low down on the northern horizon.

"There it is, by God!" he said. "The Great Circle beacon. Can you beat it? They're actually using it—in time of war!"

"Why not?" spoke up Jack Horner on his left. "They're expecting company, aren't they? Well, what do we do now? Going to land in that light?"

"Not yet, anyway!" snapped Dusty. "Maybe we won't have to land. I'm going up for altitude. Curly! Grab those night glasses in the rack there and tell me what you see. Jack—keep on that radio. I've got a hunch. Maybe we can put one over on these babies, and right under their damn noses!"

Realizing that questioning Dusty, once he got started that way, was but a waste of breath, both Curly and Jack Horner did as told. Fifteen minutes later Dusty was circling about high over the seadrome.

That it was a seadrome he knew only by the faint light shed by the revolving beacon. By peering hard he could see what looked like passenger ramps, buildings and hangars. But the center part of it seemed to be a mixture of objects that seemed to have no connection with anything else.

He gave up trying to figure it out, as Curly Brooks started to speak.

"They've done something to the center of the thing—the main runway. It looks to me like a long U-shaped trough, that extends the entire length of the seadrome. No, wait a minute—at the east end it flanges out spade shaped. What the hell could that be? The landing and take off runways are on both sides of it. And—hey, here's a couple of Darts down there or I'm a liar! I can just see them in the hangar light on the north side. They—"

He stopped short as his pal grabbed him.

"Give me those glasses and take over, Curly!"

Brooks shrugged, handed over the glasses and dropped into

the pilot's seat. Bracing himself, Dusty put the glasses to his eyes and stared downward. The seadrome seemed to leap up to him in the lenses.

It was about a mile long and half a mile wide. Save for the revolving beacon there were few lights. But as the beacon swung its beam across the seadrome, he was able to pick out the sil-

A DOUBLE ROW OF FLOODLIGHTS FLARED UP

houettes of low buildings, hangars, the passenger station and maintenance crew sleeping quarters.

But, Curly had been right. Something had been added to the center of the main take-off and landing runway. It was a U-shaped trough that was flush with the landing deck on the east side, where it flanged outward to the sides, and was gradually built up to a four or five degree angle at the western end.

ON THE SEADROME AS THEY GLIDED DOWN

Though he peered at it until his eyes ached he couldn't figure out what it could be. The thing it resembled the most was a log sluice for bringing timber down out of high mountains.

HE FORGOT about it for the minute, though, as he suddenly saw two jet-winged Darts pulled up in front of an open hangar on the north side. He didn't need two looks to know that they belonged to the Hawk's brood. Did one of them, perhaps, belong to the Hawk himself? Was that dirty rat down there?

As the question slid across his brain, he unconsciously bunched a fist and pressed it hard against the side of the cabin.

And then, suddenly, it happened.

Without warning, a giant pencil of white light shot up from the east end of the seadrome and began cutting slow circles about the sky. As Dusty stared at it dumbfounded for the fraction of a second, he saw the beam light up a flight of Darts, not a quarter of a mile away, and less than five thousand feet below him. They were flying south in V formation.

In the next split second he had turned, shoved the glasses into Curly's hands, and exchanged places.

"Whatcha going to do?" gasped Curly.

"Get the hell away from here first!" Dusty snapped back, and sent the amphibian rocketing around toward the west.

Two minutes later, he hauled the throttle all the way back, and the plane was sliding softly down through the night skies. He reached out his free hand and rapped Agent 10 on the arm.

"Jack! Never mind that a second. Listen to me. You, too, Curly. We've got to get aboard the seadrome! There's something funny down there. Now, here's the plan. Jack, get their signal station. Fake yourself as some important Black, and ask that they light up the eastern end of the seadrome. Get me—the eastern end!"

"But why?" cut in the Intelligence man. "They may get wise, may suspect!"

"Let them!" Dusty barked. "All I want is for them to concentrate on the eastern end. That will leave the western end dark. I'm going to glide us around, and hit water on the northern side, and let the run take us in close. Curly! You be set to get up and out onto the wing and fend us off as we mush in. That seadrome is forty feet high, and with luck we can get in under its shadow."

"Worth a try, anyway," grunted Brooks. "But after that, what?"

Dusty bit his lip. He hated to say the next—but he had to.

"It will be every man for himself," he said. "Stick as long as you can. But if one of us gets caught, its up to the other two to carry on. No matter who loses—we've got to wreck whatever is on that seadrome! You agree with me?"

Neither of them made an answer. There was nothing that they could say. They simply laid a hand on Dusty's arm and pressed hard.

"Thanks, fellows," said Dusty thickly. And then in steady tones to young Horner, "O.K., Jack, get going on that radio."

CHAPTER 10
THE RED DESTROYER

THERE WAS a heavy moment of silence in the cabin. Then it was broken by the sound of Agent 10's voice jabbering into the transmitter tube. Instinctively, Dusty hunched forward over the Dep wheel, and fastened his eyes on the seadrome off to his right and far below. Seconds of agonizing suspense dragged by and then, suddenly, Agent 10 stopped jabbering and let out a cry of joy.

"We made it fellows! They just O.K.'d the request."

Even as the last word ripped off the Intelligence man's lips, Dusty saw the circling pencil of light wink out and a double row of flood lights bordering the north and south side of the eastern end of the seadrome flare up. Instantly both runways were flooded with the light of day.

"Get set, Curly!" said Dusty tensely. "We're going down!"

Reaching out his free hand, he snapped off the ignition and steepened the plane's glide. Around and down he went in a wide sweeping circle that brought him rushing toward the sea drome from the north west.

Dead ahead was the great floating platform, its western end bathed in semi-darkness and its buildings at the eastern end sharply silhouetted against the glare of the flood lights. And beyond them, farther to the east, Dusty was sure that he saw the shadows of a flight of Black Darts circling slowly about.

The sight of them sent little icy chills rippling up and down his spine, and the roof of his mouth went dry. He cursed in-

126

wardly, clamped down on his jangling nerves and eased up the hull nose for a skimming landing.

Movement at his right told him that Curly was preparing to push out through the cabin ceiling trap door and work his way along the wing. Good old Curly! Set for anything, at anytime, and no questions asked. For his sake he had to make the landing perfect.

The giant seadrome was now less than sixty yards away. It seemed like a half dozen city blocks all moulded into one great square of black granite. Though only forty feet from the water to the lip it seemed to Dusty a thousand feet high.

If only he could mush the amphibian in under its over-hanging edge. Getting aboard would be simple after that. Many times had be landed upon it before war broke out. He knew that there were countless companionway stairs leading up to the main deck from the water. Hell yes, if only—

And then the hull touched water!

Instantly Dusty hauled the Dep wheel all the way back, and started to ease on the left rudder. On the corner of his eye he saw Curly climb out through the cabin door. As his pal disappeared from view, Dusty applied more left rudder. The hull turned and the amphibian started to grab sidewise, wing-on to the drome.

The next ten seconds were ten years to Dusty's life. At first he was afraid that he'd landed too soon, and that the amphibian would not have enough mush-run to take it in under the overhanging edge of the sea drome. Hell, they'd have to swim for it. And then it seemed as though they were going to smash into its great dark and looming bulk. Instinctively he jammed on full left rudder, and flung himself from the seat.

"Jack!" he whispered hoarsely. "Come on!"

His words were a waste of breath. Agent 10 was already at his side. Together they climbed up through the cabin ceiling trapdoor and out onto the water drenched wing. All about was pitch darkness. They couldn't even see their hands before their faces. Inch by inch they crawled out on the smooth metal wing that weaved slowly up and down beneath their weight.

They were halfway out when Dusty felt the plane bump into something rigid. It threw him off balance for a split second and he almost went plunging off into the water. Only lightning like action saved him a bath.

"Got it, fellows! Come on!"

CURLY'S FAINT whisper came back with the startling clearness of an exploding shell. Dusty crawled forward, and presently bumped into his pal, who was hanging half off the end of the wing and holding fast to a mooring ring attached to the bottom post of a set of companionway stairs. Dusty flattened himself, reached out and grabbed the ring, too. And together they pulled the amphibian in close.

"Couldn't have done better in daylight, kid!" came Curly's excited whisper. "We hit right smack at these stairs. Hold it a minute."

"What's the matter?" breathed Dusty, as he felt his pal's body twisting about. "What are you doing?"

"Maybe we'll want to go home in this thing!" was the answer. "I'm fixing her fast!"

Dusty grinned in the darkness. Trust Curly to have brains in the pinches! He'd brought a mooring rope from the cabin.

A minute or so later Curly touched his arm and also grabbed Agent 10.

"Set, fellows! Aboard we go!"

In Indian file, Curly first because he was the nearest, they stepped off the end of the wing and onto the companionway stairs. Hand gripping his automatic Dusty followed his pal up the stairs and onto a pitch dark level space that he realized was directly beneath the main deck. There they paused for a minute, and then Dusty took charge. He reached out and pulled them close.

"There's a way up, down to our left," he whispered. "I remember, now. It will bring us up behind the passenger station. Guns out, fellows. Each chap grab hold of the shirt of the chap in front of him. O.K.? Let's go. No wait! Remember—if we get spotted, split up."

Hands out in front of him, and eyes straining into the darkness, Dusty started slowly to the left. At the end of perhaps fifteen yards, he bumped into a steel wall. Moving off at right angles he worked his way along, one hand on the wall, until he came to a sloping ramp.

Up it he started, hugging the rail on the right side. There was a bend in the sloping ramp, and as he rounded it he saw a faint glimmer of light about him. He pulled up so quickly that Curly plowed into him with a faint grunt.

Oblivious to his pal, Dusty stared at the glimmer of light for several seconds, and then relaxed. What he was looking at was that reflection of the floodlights far down at the eastern end of the drome. He reached back, touched Curly and started up again.

Five minutes later the three of them were on the main deck and hugging the darkness of the rear wall of the passenger building on the north side of the drome.

And then, suddenly, they all froze rigid as there came the sharp sounds of footsteps along the metal deck. Footsteps that were coming directly toward them! Virtually trying to squeeze his body into the wall Dusty brought up his gun, butt first, and waited breathlessly. The footsteps came nearer. They were only about a dozen paces away.

Then without warning, they stopped.

A wild urge to fling himself forward surged through Dusty. It was with a tremendous effort that he curbed down on the desire and held himself rigid. One—two—three seconds ticked by, and then the footsteps advanced. But as they came abreast of where Dusty and his pals crouched, they stopped again.

And in the next second a thin beam of white light cut the darkness and splashed straight into their faces.

Dusty was hardly conscious that he moved. Instinct, and nothing else, had made him fling himself forward, gun upraised. He brought it down with all his might. A wild cry blasted against his ear-drums. A spurt of red and yellow flame seemed to spew starlight into his face. And the roar of a gun shook the air.

Unable to see for the moment, he was nevertheless conscious of his gun butt crashing down on something solid. What it hit

130

reeled back, slammed into the guard rail of the deck and cart-wheeled over it and down into the water.

LIGHTS WERE beginning to spring up all over now. And in the distance came the hoarse shouting of voices. Dusty spun around to his pals.

"Split!" he snapped, "Work along to the hangar on the northeast corner. Luck, fellows!"

There was no time for hand-shakes, even though they had felt that way. Darting to his left, Dusty sped across the deck and slid over the guard rail. Hanging by one hand he reached down with the other, got a good grip on the lip of the scuppers and let his body slowly drop. Swinging like a pendulum over the water below, he closed his eyes tight for an instant and battled against the pain of the powder burn on his right cheek.

Presently he started working his way hand over hand to his left. His arms felt as though they were being pulled out of their sockets by the weight of his body.

The blood began to pound against his temples, and little pinwheels of fire spun around in front of his eyes. A hundred times he was positive that he couldn't hold on any longer. And a hundred times the fighting instinct within him refused to quit and forced him onward.

Eventually, it seemed like a thousand years later, his legs bumped into a small platform that projected out from the side of the seadrome. It was the platform used for unloading supplies of fuel from tankers and the one thing he had, been banking his hopes upon reaching. Pulling up his knees he swung himself up onto the platform and let go.

For a moment or two he lay in a huddled heap, biting his lips against the sharp pains that shot up and down both arms. Presently, though, he forced himself to his hands and knees, crawled across the platform and wiggled in through the half opened loading port.

Darkness, thicker than ever, engulfed him. He reached out both hands and felt the slick sides of oil drums, Grabbing hold of one he pulled himself to his feet, and stood there listening intently.

At first he heard nothing. The shouting had died down, and it seemed as though the entire seadrome was deserted of all humans save himself. His heart looped over as he thought of Agent 10 and Curly—particularly Curly. Jack Horner was in the guise of a Black. He knew their language and their customs. Chances of him being caught were practically nil as compared to Curly's.

What a hell of a foolish idea anyway? A hunch, a bit of unconfirmed information, and he had dragged his two best pals into a network of mystery and death. Far better that he'd tried it alone.

"Cut it, kid!" he grated at himself. "You know damn well that Curly wanted it as much as you did!"

The thought, though he didn't try to analyze it, gave him a certain amount of comfort. Then he banished it from his mind and started to feel his way among the oil drums. And then suddenly he stiffened motionless.

From somewhere far ahead, toward the eastern end of the

sea drome, came a low throbbing sound. First impression was that it was a plane being reved up.

But as he strained his ears, he detected a strange skipping note. It was something like the back-fire of a low powered automobile engine. Yet, on second thought, it wasn't. It was spaced at regular intervals between series of throbbing notes.

He moved off in that direction. A moment later his groping hands touched a steel door. He fumbled for the handle, turned it and pulled the door open. The throbbing sound grew louder as he paused on the threshold and stared into more darkness. Moving slowly, and feeling every foot of the way with both his hands and his feet, he traveled across a metal floor. Three times he bumped into what felt like packing cases.

He didn't stop to explore. The throbbing sound, with its strange skipping note, was growing louder with each passing second. It seemed to be coming from more to the left than the right. He veered left and a few minutes later discovered the reason. On the sea side of the storeroom, in which he guessed himself to be, there was a long narrow corridor that lead along the outside of the seadrome.

HESITATING BUT a moment to pull the automatic he had jammed into his pocket before leaping for the guard rail, he stepped into the corridor and started swiftly along it.

As he guided himself by keeping one outstretched hand on the inside wall, he felt several doors that lead off to other underside parts of the drome. But he didn't pause to go through any of them. The throbbing sound was so loud now that it seemed that he would come upon it at any moment.

And then, without warning he walked slam-bang into a solid wall at the far end of the corridor. He cursed softly, retraced his steps until he felt the nearest door, and put his ear against it.

The result was a tingle of excitement slicing through him. The door against which his ear was pressed lead to the strange throbbing sound. It couldn't possibly lead anywhere else. The sound was as clear as though it came from the metal of the door itself.

Sliding down his free hand he gripped the knob and turned it, a prayer on his lips. The prayer was answered immediately. The door gave to the pressure of his hand and moved slowly inward. He stopped when it was open an inch, and put his eye to the crack.

If he expected to see anything important he was completely disappointed. He found himself staring in a dimly lighted room filled with everything from coils of rope to the spare parts of airplane engines.

On the far side was another door. Boldly he stepped inside, made his way around the piles of miscellaneous equipment and over to the far door. He put his ear against it for but a split second. That was long enough. The vibration caused by the throbbing sound beyond hurt his ear-drums.

Again he reached down for the knob, and again his prayer was answered as he put his eye to the inch crack. As he squinted through, his heart seemed to leap up into his throat, and the blood in his veins to become liquid fire.

He found himself staring into a great shed-like room with a greasy shaft of steel in each of the four corners. The eastern wall was made up of what seemed to be a huge ventilator. The roof was domed-shaped, like that of any ordinary hangar, and from its giant girders were suspended long steel chains that were more like six-inch flat steel bands.

But all that he gave but one swift glance. The main thing, in fact the one and only thing that caught and held his glance, was a gigantic, queer looking object that was resting in a U-shaped trough cradle in the center of the floor.

At first it looked like a great steel shell painted a glistening red. But as he gaped at it in dumbfounded amazement, he noted individual features of the strange thing. From a pointed nose it swelled out to a diameter of perhaps twenty feet for a distance of perhaps half of its fifty-or sixty-foot length. At that point its diameter became slightly smaller and tapered down to ten-foot thickness where it flanged out cone-shaped.

From one end to the other there was not a single bump or projection in the curving lines of the thing. Just back from the nose there were what appeared to be a circle of windows. But they were not glass windows and they were absolutely flush with the surface.

So startling was the sight of the thing that for several seconds Dusty didn't realize that the queer throbbing sound was coming from the cone-shaped end.

As he switched his eyes that way again he noted that the huge ventilator was sucking pale, milkish smoke out of the room. And a moment later he became conscious of a faint acrid smell in the air he was breathing.

AND THEN, suddenly, the throbbing sound died out with

a sort of swishing whir. An instant later a small section of the side of the weird contraption dropped down, and a grease-smeared Black mechanic slid out feet first and dropped onto the floor of the shed.

Standing with his back to Dusty, the mechanic pulled a wad of waste from his jumper pockets and wiped his hands. That done with, he moved off to the right and out of line of Dusty's vision.

Heart thumping madly against his ribs, Dusty waited perhaps thirty seconds and then slowly edged the door open far enough to admit his body.

Gun gripped tightly in his right hand he slipped through and closed the door behind him. Crouching down he darted a quick look in the direction the mechanic had taken. All he saw was a wall with a door in its lower center. The door was closed.

A second in which to clamp down on his nerves, and he slid across the floor, climbed up on the U-shaped cradle and grabbed hold of the section that had dropped down. He saw instantly that it was made of some kind of metal—something like steel with criss-cross gray lines on its smoothed surface.

It was then that he also noticed why the section had not dropped onto the floor. It was hinged at the bottom. In other words, it was like the drop exit that one sees in the modern dirigibles.

Pushing with both feet, he heaved himself up onto the section and wiggled inside. At first all was darkness about him. And then as his eyes focused to the faint glow of a bug light above his head, he found himself looking at a conglomeration of objects, all of which seemed to be attached to the walls and floor of a small square compartment by heavy coiled springs.

He studied the first that met his eye. It was a bucket seat, similar to the bucket seat of a plane. Its main difference though was that it was braced by heavy coiled springs on all sides, and wide mesh straps were attached to the seat itself.

There were two seats in fact—side by side. Between them was a six-inch column secured to the floor. Its top spread out bell shaped, and on its surface were three rows of throttles, five throttles to each row.

Four feet in front of it was a third spring-braced seat that faced the forward wall a foot or so away. On the wall was a large panel covered with every type of instrument. And as Dusty slid forward for a closer look, he noted that the instruments in the lower half of the panel all had to do with gas rocket regulation, and power volume.

The top instruments were the usual speed, altitude, wind drift, electro-magnetic compass, climb and turn indicator, etc. One thing about them, though, that caused him to suck in his breath sharply, was that each dial was graduated about twenty times as much as the ordinary airplane instrument.

The top reading on the speed indicator, for instance, was in four figures.

As he stared at them, an object in the exact center of the board caught his eye. It was like two glass discs, with a felt lined shield covering the top and both sides. On sudden impulse he bent over and put his eyes to the discs.

The result caused his heart to loop over He was looking out

the forward end of the weird craft. Looking out through a tiny slit about three feet back from the tip of the blunt nose. Directly ahead he could see the forward wall with its door.

AND THEN it happened.

The handle of the door turned the door opened, and Curly Brooks stepped inside.

A cry of joy rushed up to Dusty's lips, but died instantly. Curly Brooks was not alone. Behind him walked a big Black soldier. And behind him—the Black Hawk!

It was then that Dusty really saw Curly's face. The right side was smeared with blood. The other side, ashen grey from spent effort and fatigue. Arms swinging limply at his sides, he shuffled forward as though in a daze, the soldier behind him prodding him in the back with his gun.

Rigid, Dusty watched until they passed out of view on his right. Spinning around he darted past the spring braced chairs to the opening and risked a quick look. The trio were headed toward the door through which he had entered. He waited for a split second until they were back to him, then leaped out onto the floor.

"Hold it, rats—or I'll drill you!"

His voice echoed and re-echoed about the room, and their effect was instantaneous. Both Blacks whirled. The soldier snapped up his gun. A flash dart to the side and Dusty fired. The Black didn't even have time to pull the trigger.

A steel slug from Dusty's gun slapped square into his gapping mouth and plowed right on through the base of his brain. The man was dead before he even started falling to the floor.

It all happened in the flash of a second, and before the Black Hawk could whip his hand up to his own gun Dusty was on his feet and advancing toward him.

"Draw, damn you!" he barked. "Draw! I'll even give you first shot!"

The Hawk stiffened instantly, his gun hand dropping to his side. But there was no fear in his ugly face. Only a look of snarling hatred.

"You are walking to your death, Captain Ayres. Even killing me will not save you. We knew that you were aboard —and you will never leave—alone!"

The last word jerked Dusty's eyebrows up.

"Going to keep me company?" he grinned, reaching out and unholstering the Black's gun. "Or what?"

The Black simply smiled. Dusty took his eyes off him just long enough to shoot a snap-look at Brooks who stood glassy-eyed, rocking slowly back and forth on the balls of his feet.

"Curly! Out of it, fellow—pronto!"

Brooks' eyes blinked stupidly.

"Huh? Oh, it's you, Dusty. I—look—look out!"

Dusty spun and flung up one arm, as a blurred shadow rushed toward him. He knew that he had fired his gun. He heard its roar and—

And then the whole room collapsed in on top of him.

CHAPTER 11
BLACK ULTIMATUM

WHEN DUSTY next opened his eyes, he was conscious of only one thing—someone was smashing a sledge hammer against the top of his skull. Smashing two blows to the second. He groaned, closed his eyes and tried to force his body to move. In some strange way he realized that he was lying flat on his back. He tried to roll over and couldn't.

He opened his eyes again and stared up at a pale yellow eye. It took him a full minute of painful concentration to realize that he was staring at a light. Another minute later a shadow passed over the light, and his eyes gaped at the blurred features of a human face.

"Dusty, old pal! Are you hurt bad, kid?"

The voice of Curly Brooks! The words were like a tonic to Dusty's reeling senses. His brain cleared just a wee bit. Not much, but enough for him to gather the strength to push himself up to a sitting position.

The effort made his head seem to virtually bounce up and down on his shoulders. Bracing his hands palm downward on the floor, he bit his lower lip until the blood trickled back in his mouth. Presently, a long, long presently, the dark abyss that yawned before him faded away like a lost mirage, and the kneeling figure of Curly Brooks became clear.

He stared at his pal, and grinned bitterly.

"Chalk one up for Snappy Ayres, Curly!" he grated. "God will I never learn to keep eyes in the back of my head?"

140

"The two of us, Dusty!" he said. "If I hadn't been so damn blind I would have seen that Black Rat sneaking up on you, sooner."

Dusty touched the top of his head and groaned. It was as though the skull had been ripped away and he was touching his exposed brain. He gaped about the room. There was nothing to see except four bare steel walls, and a steel door on the opposite side. He let his eyes wander back to Curly's face.

"What happened to you?" he asked. "And where are we—do you know?"

Curly glared down at the floor.

"If you think you're a sap," he gritted, "just listen to this! I sneaked around the corner of the passenger building, cut across the open deck, and—and ran right smack into the waiting arms of two Blacks! Got one of them, but the other crowned me, and how! The next thing I was really conscious of was that Black sneaking up on you. My God, what a help I am!"

"And where are we?" Dusty repeated quickly, as Curly's voice broke.

"Somewhere under the rear end of the main deck," came the low answer. "I don't know just where. After you dropped, the Black covered me. Then a couple of more came in, dragged us both away, and threw us in here. That's all I know, kid. Know anything yourself?"

To keep up his pal's hopes Dusty told him of what he had seen. But in the back of his brain he was meanwhile thinking furiously of other things. First, why the Hawk had let them both live? Secondly, where was Jack Horner? Had he been captured, too?

"God, then that was the thing they call the Red Destroyer!"

Curly's voice came to him out of a thought fog. He gaped at his pal.

"Huh? What was I saying?"

"Telling me about that thing you saw—the controls and instruments. Good God, do you suppose it really flies?"

Dusty nodded.

"Yes," he said. "I read an article about that type of craft, oh, three or four years ago. It was only the theory of a haywire scientist then. His claim was, 'Give me power enough and I'll fly a billiard table!' He believed that sufficient directionally controlled gas rocket driving force could push anything through the air, regardless of lifting surface. In other words, he maintained that the perfect aircraft was simply a streamlined cabin, with no wings, and unlimited directional gas rocket driving force."

"Clear as mud!" grunted Curly, as Dusty paused and gingerly touched his head again. "But, you don't mean that that things goes through buildings, and sinks battle cruisers?"

Dusty's head was hurting too much to continue his technical discourse.

"Something like that," he grunted, and changed the subject. "Do you know where Jack is, Curly? Did he go with you?"

Brooks shook his head.

"I didn't see him again, after you said for us to split. He faded, clean. God, I hope he isn't caught. He—"

DUSTY SUDDENLY shot out his hand and clamped it

over his pal's lips. Brooks mumbled something, then seeing the look in Dusty's eyes shut up and screwed around on the floor.

The door in the steel wall was opening. A moment later three armed Blacks and the Hawk stepped inside. He stopped and smiled at them. It was not a pleasant smile.

"You have recovered, I see. Good! I was afraid that perhaps my men had struck too hard."

"No!" Dusty clipped back at him.

The Hawk held his smile and said nothing. Then he motioned to the two guards. Dusty saw the heavy rope they carried, as they advanced toward him. He bunched his fists, and braced himself to spring up. Then relaxed almost immediately. It was foolish to try it. He'd only get another clout on the head for his efforts.

Gritting his teeth, he allowed them to jerk him to his feet and bind his hands and arms tightly behind his back. Then he stood swaying as they jerked up Curly and did likewise.

"Sorry to inconvenience you, captain," came the Hawk's harsh voice. "But past experience has proven that you are exceedingly quick with your hands."

Dusty looked at him, unblinking.

"That's right," he said. "They've found your jaw more than once to good purpose. "You're getting bright."

The Hawk laughed.

"Not half as bright as you will soon realize, captain!"

Without waiting for Dusty's next comment, he jabbered off a snarling order at the three soldiers. Two of them seized Dusty

143

and Curly, and as the third pulled up in the rear, the entire party marched out the door and down a long corridor.

At its end they turned and went down a short flight of steel steps, turned sharply left and through another door.

It was the door through which Curly and the Hawk had entered. Once inside the room Dusty snapped his eyes to the Red Destroyer. The section was still hanging down on its hinges, and there was no throbbing sound coming from the cone-shaped end.

And then as his eyes traveled to the left he checked his pace unconsciously, and swallowed hard. On the left side of the room, standing straddle-legged, and arms folded on his mighty chest was none other than Fire-Eyes, commander in chief of the Black Invaders.

The guard hurled Dusty forward. He stumbled and would have fallen flat on his face at the feet of Fire-Eyes but for some mighty quick footwork, and the fact that his guard did not let go of him entirely. Straightening up he stared expressionless up at the blazing orbs behind the two slits in the green mask.

Presently a voice boomed out from behind that mask.

"Our guest again I see, captain. You were saying something yesterday about hoping to meet me, were you not?"

Dusty said nothing. Words rose to his lips, but the choked them back. Fire-Eyes had not had Curly and himself brought here before him to gloat. The giant behind that mask had something else in mind—something very definite. He could feel it in the very atmosphere. And for that reason he kept his mouth shut. Let Fire-Eyes do all the talking, damn his rotten black heart.

And Fire-Eyes started to. His deep voice pounded around the room like a dozen foghorns going full blast.

"And your friend Lieutenant Brooks is with us, too! A very nice little party, we shall have. One that I am positive you will remember—as long as you live!"

There was a startled gasp at Dusty's side. He half turned his head. Curly Brooks was gapping wide eyed at Fire-Eyes. It was the first time that the lean pilot had met the Black commander in the flesh, and the expression on his face showed it.

"Don't stare, kid!" grunted Dusty. "It's rude, you know!"

"Silence!"

At first Dusty thought that someone had fired a battleship salvo, so great was the roar that came from behind the green mask. And it continued.

"Silence! Do you hear me?"

The words came off Dusty's lips before he could check them.

"Yes, but only just barely."

FIRE-EYES DROPPED his folded arms to his sides, and took a step forward. Dusty saw the huge gauntleted fists bunch and inwardly braced himself for the blow. But it never came. The Black commander stopped short, and seemed to shrug. He spoke again, and his voice was almost human.

"You are interested in this, our Red Destroyer, captain?" he asked. "Rather a marked advance in aeronautical science, yes."

Dusty turned and stared at the shell-shaped craft. He was

near the nose, and for the first time he was able to get a close view of the circle of flush windows.

As he looked at them he realized that they were not windows at all. Rather they were honeycombed squares of rocket gas vents. Knowledge of that brought instant realization of how the craft was controlled in the air. Speed was produced by the large cone-shaped rocket vent at the tail.

But directional control was obtained with these forward gas vents. Gas rocket force from the underneath one sent the craft upward, and rocket force from the top vent tilted the nose down. The idea was the same with relation to the vents on either side.

He turned back to Fire-Eyes.

"Not much," he said. "It's old stuff. What else is on your mind?"

The instant the last word slid off his lips a steel fist smashed against his left temple. He reeled sidewise, the inside of his head clanging like a four-alarm fire gong. A murky sea of dizziness swirled up to him, and it took every last ounce of savage will-power to remain erect.

"Swine!" the Hawk's hissing voice smote his ear-drums. "You will treat the High Commander with the utmost of respect!"

Dusty turned and fixed agate eyes on the cruel featured face.

"That's one I owe you!" he grated.

The Hawk snarled, raised his clenched fist again, but dropped it instantly as Fire-Eyes thundered at him in his own language. Standing ramrod, the Hawk pulled the queer salute of the Invaders—right hand raised upward in line with the right shoulder and palm forward—and then stepped back. Dusty nodded at Fire-Eyes.

"Thanks for that, anyway," he said evenly.

The Black commander grunted.

"You need not thank me for anything, Captain Ayres," he said. "And now, since you seem disinterested in the Red Destroyer—notwithstanding what it has already done—we will turn to other things. Where is this spy known as Agent 10?"

"Huh? Where's who? "Dusty came right back. "I don't get you."

As he spoke the words in his heart were pounding and his brain was racing. So that was it; That was why he and Curly still lived. Jack was still undiscovered. And these tramps were getting more worried by the minute.

"I repeat my question!" boomed Fire-Eyes. "Where is Agent 10? He accompanied you on this fool's journey."

"My guess," said Dusty evenly, "is that Agent 10 is somewhere near H-Six. By the way, he needs target practice I guess. Or did he hit you?"

The Black commander did not answer for a moment. Though Dusty was not sure, lie thought he saw the black uniformed figure go rigid.

"It was not Agent 10, but one of his confederates, who tried to shoot me," Fire-Eyes replied suddenly. "Fool that he was, he died. You are lying to me, captain. Agent 10 came with you! He is here on this seadrome in the disguise of one of our race!"

Dusty shrugged.

"Then why ask me?"

147

THE GUARD HURLED
DUSTY FORWARD

"Where is your plane?"

The Black commander boomed out the words, and it was with tremendous effort that Dusty kept his face straight. They hadn't found the plane, yet. And probably wouldn't until daylight. God, if only Jack Horner could—

"Answer me—and the truth!"

Dusty made a wry face.

"O.K.," he said. "You have mussed me up enough for one day. The plane is on its way back to America. You see, Curly and I don't count. We just gambled, and I guess we lose. But the information that the pilot of that plane is taking back to America—counts a whole lot!"

As he finished, the Hawk darted forward, saluted his superior, and started jabbering. For two or three minutes they kept up a rapid-fire conversation. Then the Hawk saluted again, and turned to Dusty. His lips were curled back in a triumphant smile that revealed his ugly fang-like teeth.

"So the plane is on its way back to America, eh?" he leered. "Your bluff is as clear as glass. You see, captain, I happen to know quite definitely that Agent 10 is not a pilot!"

Dusty gave him the leveled eye.

"Who said he was, sweetheart?"

"You did!—by the admission that the third member of your foolish raiding party was flying the plane back. And that third member is Agent 10. Ah, no more bluff, captain! It was Agent 10 who sent those misleading messages to us. Exactly—because Agent 10 is the one man who knows our language sufficient enough for that. Now, dog—where is he?"

149

"I don't know," Dusty snapped. "Why not look for him?"

And as the Hawk's mouth started to pop open, he added, "At H-6! That was the last we heard of him."

The Hawk started to speak again, but Fire-Eyes reached out and pushed him to one side. The eyes he fixed on Dusty seemed to blaze up more than ever.

"**I WILL** put it this way, Captain Ayres," he began. "It is possible for us to find Agent 10, but it would take time. And time we cannot waste right now, unless it is imperative that we do so. You see, your President has given me no reply, and there is work to do. So, to avoid any unnecessary waste of time, I ask you for the last time—where is Agent 10? Is he aboard?"

Dusty hesitated, stuck his jaw out.

"And I tell you for the first time," he replied in a hard voice, "go jump in the ocean!"

Breathless silence settled over the room for perhaps five seconds. Out the corner of his eye Dusty saw the Black Hawk swaying toward him. Stark murder was written all over the man's face. But Dusty knew that he would not leap. He feared the consequences, should his superior not "cotton" to the idea.

"So?" Fire-Eyes roared out suddenly. "You refuse to answer, eh? Very well, captain, I once made you answer my questions. And I am sure that I can repeat!"

Turning his masked face from Dusty the Black commander bellowed an order at one of the guards. The man turned instantly and ran over to one corner of the room. He grabbed hold of the handle of a lever, that Dusty saw for the first time, and pulled it toward him.

From under the floor of the room there came a low whirring sound, like a dynamo starting up. Presently the floor quivered. And then, as Dusty sucked in his breath sharply, the entire floor began to rise.

Instinctively his eyes snapped over to the steel column in each corner. A flash glance was all he needed. The entire shed was an elevator, and the steel columns were guideways for raising and lowering it.

Slowly but surely the shed rose higher and higher. Its dome roof cleared the main deck and cool sea air rushed in. Higher it went, until Dusty found himself staring at the U-shaped trough that ran the entire length of the seadrome.

The floodlights had gone out, but sunken deck lights made it possible for him to see everything. Once again he had the impression that he was looking at a lumber sluice. But as he gazed intently he saw that every fifteen or twenty feet of the trough had a trip cable, such as is used on airplane carriers for bringing landing planes to a sure and quick stop.

Sight of the trip cables, now slack in the trough, and memory of how the eastern end of the trough flanged out spade shaped, answered the last performance question that had been lingering in the back of his brain.

Getting the Red Destroyer into the air he understood perfectly. The mile long U-trough, that he now noted was constructed of a green metal, was enough for the craft to generate full power—the four or five degree uplift being sufficient to get altitude without using the lower rocket force vents.

And now as he saw it, he realized that landing the terrifically fast craft was just as simple. The flanged rear end, which was a part of the shed roof, allowed for miscalculation on the part of the pilot and widened his landing area. No matter how he entered, his craft would be guided into the trough and eventually stopped by the trip-cables. Because everything in the operating compartment was spring-braced, the occupants would experience no more jar than that of the ordinary landing.

In fact, they probably didn't experience any jolt—considering that the craft's purpose was to plow through stone and steel-girdered buildings.

Turning around, Dusty found himself staring out over open sea. The elevator was really a movable platform. The walls of the room were solid fixtures below.

Turning front again he stared absently at the landing deck and the assortment of hangars and buildings that flanked both sides. Save for the U-shaped trough, he had often viewed the scene in times of peace. And now it was a death nest in the hands of blood-thirsty killers.

"Now, captain, watch carefully, please."

The voice of Fire-Eyes made Dusty jerk around. He looked at the Black commander and saw him motion to the Hawk. The Hawk in turn motioned to the guards, and grated out a few words. Instantly the guards grabbed Curly Brooks, cut the ropes from his arms and heaved him helplessly up on their shoulders.

"Damn you!" howled Dusty starting forward.

He took but one step. The huge hand of Fire-Eyes swept out and knocked him flat on the deck.

"You will only watch, captain!" came the roaring voice.

HALF BLIND with rage, Dusty struggled to his feet again, only to have one of the guards jab the muzzle of a gun into the small of his back. Helpless, he watched the other two guards sling Curly spread-eagle over the nose of the Red Destroyer and lash him fast with lengths of steel wire.

"Of course he will not remain there long, you understand, captain," said the voice of Fire-Eyes behind him. "The terrific speed will pull him off. However, it is possible that he may be there when the Red Destroyer reaches your nation's capital!"

The words were like swords of fire passing through Dusty's brain. From miles away he heard his own roaring voice.

"You devils—take him down, or by God I'll smoke you out in hell!"

"You will answer my question, captain?"

The voice, so close was it, seemed to blast Dusty's ear-drums right into his head.

"Go to the devil!" he thundered.

A jabbered order clattered out from behind the mask. The Black Hawk and one of the guards, ran around to the side of the Red Destroyer and climbed inside. Another guard started turning a crank at the right front end of the cradle.

A moment later the cradle slid slowly forward until it was flush with the U-shaped trough.

And then there came a throbbing sound and the deck shook beneath Dusty's feet. Through blurred eyes he saw pale vapor spurt out from the gas rocket vents in the nose. Curly was two feet in front of them, but his body twitched violently.

That was more than Dusty could stand. The inside of his head seemed to explode.

"Wait—wait!" he bellowed. "I'll answer your question!"

CHAPTER 12
T.N.T. EAGLE

IN TWO long strides, Fire-Eyes reached the opening in the side of the Red Destroyer. He thundered an order, and instantly the throbbing sound died away. Turning back, he bent his blazing orbs down on Dusty.

"Well?" he boomed. "Speak!"

"Dusty—damn you—keep your trap closed! The hell with the bums!"

The voice of Curly Brooks was little more than a hoarse whisper. Dusty bit his lip, hesitated. To save Curly was to betray Jack Horner. Both were his pals. Both were fighting the same battle as he. And both, just as he, stood ready to sacrifice themselves on the altar of everlasting peace for a world gone mad with blood, and death, and war.

The life of one man was unimportant. The situation was one that dealt with the lives of thousands—yes, millions.

"For the last time—speak! Speak, or before your very eyes you will see your friend's body dissolve and become nothing. In those rocket vents is also an acid that becomes flame once it reaches the air—a flame that can even burn through this steel deck upon which you now stand. Speak—or your friend shall feel that flame!"

Desperately Dusty tried to gather his whirling senses. A crazy quirk in his brain was linking up the last words of Fire-Eyes with the fate of the *Utah, Texas* and *Vermont*. So, what the charge of the Red Destroyer had not done, the steel-eating flame had!

"Tell him to go to hell, Dusty!" Curly shouted.

Dusty looked at Fire-Eyes, and nodded slowly.

"You win," he said quietly. "I—Wait a minute—I think I'm passing out."

He stumbled to the side, and forced himself to cough raspingly. Then he slowly straightened up.

"Thanks, for waiting," he gulped. "Well, here's the whole damn truth, Agent 10—"

He never finished. Even as the words came off his lips, he whirled, put his head down and smashed square into the stomach of the Black Hawk, who had come out of the Red Destroyer to listen.

The man roared with rage, and flung up both his hands. But the Yank had come at him like a battering-ram, and he went over on his back like a sack of meal. Without even checking his pace, Dusty streaked zigzag across the deck and tore around the corner of the passenger building.

Behind him guns cracked, and voices roared; most of the drowned out by the mighty bellowing of Fire-Eyes. Unseen metallic wasps twanged past him. One of them cut a stinging gash across his left shoulder.

Zigzagging at top speed he ran blindly along, the passageway behind the passenger building. His arms still bound behind his back retarded him greatly, but he put everything he had into it and whirled around a second corner. Twenty feet in front of him was one of the many ramps leading down to the lower level.

He didn't run down it. He hurled his body forward, twisted sidewise in midair and landed on the slope on his side. And down he rolled, over, and over, and over.

A buzz-saw was chewing through his brain, and a trip-hammer was pounding an unmerciful tattoo against every square inch of his body. And then he crashed into something solid and stopped rolling.

Half-conscious, he lay gasping for breath. But suddenly, as a renewed roar of voices came to his ears, he stumbled to his feet and staggered forward in the inky darkness.

At the end of twenty steps, something slammed into his face. It was a wall. Turning back to it, he slid sidewise rubbing its surface with his bound hands.

The voices came nearer and nearer. He groaned and moved faster until he found the door. Hitching himself up on his toes he fumbled for the knob, just managed to get it between his fingers, and turned it by gripping hard and leaning his body to the side.

Letting go of it he stepped through into another pit of darkness, without wasting time to close it tight, he plunged straight forward.

As he did his knee crashed into something and he went flat. His head struck steel deck.

"Up—up, you damn fool! You've got to keep going!"

The words were but a whispered gurgle in his throat. Gritting his teeth he wiggled and wrenched up on his knees, and then up onto his feet. His legs were like lead pipes, and there was no feeling in his arms. His heart was pounding so hard, that it seemed to beat every drop of air out of his lungs. But forward he went again, only to stumble and crash into more invisible objects.

How big the room was, and what it contained, he had no idea. And less, of where he might find the door. Dully he could hear pounding footsteps above him. In fact some of them seemed to come from the room he'd just left.

A MOMENT later, that suspicion was confirmed. Voice rang out and the reflection from a beam of light seeped into the room. But, though at first it turned his heart to ice, a second later it flooded his entire body with wild hope.

In the moment the reflection remained, he saw a great pile of loose heap not a dozen feet from him. It consisted of countless frayed ends of mooring ropes, tossed carelessly in the corner to await shipment to somewhere for recombing and weaving. Undoubtedly it was the accumulation of years—years before the war began.

Fired by that hope, sight and action became one. Dusty hurled himself toward it and slumped down on the floor. Flat on his back he swiveled around and shoved his head under it. Then turning over so that his bound hands were against the wall, he shoved with them, and dug into the floor and wall with the heels of his boots.

Inch by inch he worked his way under the great pile of

thready, fluffy stuff. It got in his eyes and mouth to almost stifle him. But he simply gritted his teeth and inched in deeper. His head bumping against the corner wall told him that he was completely covered. But to make sure he arched his back and jackknifed his knees into his stomach.

Seconds dragged by and became minutes.

Suddenly, he heard Black voices close by. He opened his eyes and noted a faint yellow blur sweeping about above him. An instant later the pile of hemp shivered and shook. Someone was kicking and prodding about in it.

A spear of fire slid down across his left thigh. It was all he could do to stop from gasping. A bayonet had just grazed his leg. Another inch to the left, and it would have sliced to the bone, and the man holding the bayonet known that he had struck something besides loose hemp.

Eyes closed, body motionless as that of a corpse, Dusty waited for the next thrust—the thrust that would probably cut deep into his face, or perhaps drive right through his chest. No second thrust reached him. And after what seemed an eternity of hell the dull glow moving about the top of the hemp, disappeared, and footsteps retreated rapidly across the metal floor.

Slowly, drop by drop, Dusty eased the clamped air out of his aching lungs. For the first time he realized there was a sharp pain in his left hand.

He moved both hands away and the pain stopped. Then he moved them back and groped with his fingers as much as his bound wrists would allow.

He was touching the jagged edge of a crimped deck plate

that did not fit flush with the wall. At some time or another, a table, perhaps, or a bench had been riveted there. It had been removed and the edge of the deck plate had been twisted upward.

Even as he speculated as to what had once occupied that particular corner, he was wiggling his body around so that the ropes that bound his arms were pressing against the sharp edge.

And then began a session of hitching his body up and down, that drenched him from head to foot with salty sweat, and wracked his body with numbing pain. But finally two of the strands gave, and he felt the others slacken. Freeing himself entirely was but the matter of a minute or two.

Pulling his arms out from under him, he paused long enough to rub back partial-circulation, and then slowly pushed himself up to a sitting position.

That accomplished, he got slowly up on his knees, and with both hands began pushing the hemp aside. Finally he was clear of it; on his feet and leaning against the wall, sucking in lungful after lungful of blessed clean air.

As soon as new strength began to flood back into his body he started forward in the darkness, hands out in front of him. His left leg was stiff and pained him a lot. But after feeling the gash with his fingers and convincing himself that his breeches had suffered far more damage than the flesh of his leg, he dismissed it from his mind, and continued to feel his way about the various objects in the room.

As in another room, they seemed to be miscellaneous packing cases, bound with metal strips.

Presently he reached the far side of the room, found the door, fumbled for the knob—and met a set-back. It was locked tight, and there was no key in the lock.

He reversed his direction and worked his way back across the room to the door through which he had originally entered. It opened at his touch. He slid through it and crouched motionless.

Ahead of him he could just barely see the ramp leading up to the main deck. To his left was blank steel wall. But as he stared to the right, he saw the faint outlines of two doors, and immediately realized why the searching Black had not spent much time in the room behind him.

Dusty could just as well have escaped through either one of three doors.

For ten seconds or more he stared at them. Then, on impulse, moved over to the one on the right. Holding his breath he jammed an ear against it and listened intently. Not a sound came from beyond.

Cautiously he curled his fingers over the knob, twisted and pushed forward. Half an inch was enough. He was looking into a long passageway that ran transversely across the seadrome. He was about to step through, when suddenly he stiffened.

A BLACK guard had stepped out from some other room, about fifty yards down the passageway—and was coming his way.

He closed the door softly, and stood motionless. Then he darted to the right and flattened himself against the wall.

The wait was less than half a minute. The door made a

clicking sound, swung open to shed faint yellow light into dark places, and a Black-uniformed figure stepped through.

The man's foot hadn't even touched the deck when Dusty slashed over with his clenched right fist. In the practically infinitesimal period of time that it took that clenched ball of steel to travel the two feet, the Black jerked his head around. But that's all he did—just jerked his head around.

Dusty's fist caught him on the jaw with a sharp smacking sound. The Black blinked twice, and his knees gave way. Darting in, Dusty caught him and let him touch the floor gently.

The first thing he did was to relieve the Black of his gun. And the second thing was to relieve the Black of his uniform. Three minutes later he had pulled it on over his own, and, gun in hand, was stepping through the door into the corridor.

For a moment he had been inclined to go back on the main deck by way of the ramp. But he killed the idea as too risky. The passageway seemed to lead straight across the seadrome. If it did, he might be able to circle back to the Red Destroyer in the opposite direction from which he had escaped.

Like a shadow he moved down the dimly-lighted passage. He passed three or four doors without even giving them a single glance. His eyes were fixed on the door at the far end.

Suddenly, he stopped dead in his tracks, and stood listening. From above him and far to the left came the throbbing sound with its strange skipping note.

"My God, Curly!" he gasped, and started running toward the far door.

He never reached it.

161

When he was fifty feet away, it burst open and two Black soldiers charged in. There was no time for him to duck into any of the side doors. The Blacks saw him instantly; saw his face and realized in a flash.

Their gun hands snapped up as one. Dusty flung himself flat and pulled the trigger of his gun. And a split second later the passageway roared with sound.

Through a blur Dusty saw one of the Blacks throw up his hands, spin around twice and crash down on his face. The other Black ducked down and fired.

Something hissed past Dusty's face, and went twanging down the metal passageway. He rolled completely over, shoved out his gun and jerked the trigger. Two roars mingled into one, and an invisible hand snatched Dusty's black skull cap from his head.

But he didn't even know it. He was conscious only of the second Black. The man had jerked up straight. His gun was held straight out in front of him. But he could not pull the trigger. Couldn't, because of a tiny blue hole right smack in the middle of his forehead, out of which trickled a tiny drop of red blood. For perhaps half a second he remained just like that, and then, stiff as a log, he fell over on his back.

Dusty didn't wait to see him hit. Beyond the end door were shouting voices.

He took a swift look in back of him. The nearest side door was fifteen feet away. Seeing it was action. He spun, made the door in two cat-like leaps and grabbed the knob.

There was no time to be cautious now. He shoved the door

open and leaped through, gun out in front of him as he let his body fall to the side, and kicked the door shut.

Subconsciously expecting to hear the crash of a gun, he swept the room with his eyes. A single light burned in the ceiling. Its faint glow filtered down on a collection of objects, none of which were human beings. As he stared at them, he suddenly realized that he was cold. It was as though he had burst inside a refrigerating room. A moment later he realized that was exactly what he had done—burst into a refrigerating room.

But it wasn't the dry coldness that made him step back instinctively. It was the row after row of metal cases, open at the top, and filled with sawdust and shredded mohair. He had seen similar cases many times at American arsenals and ammo depots.

In other words, the room in which he stood was an ammo storeroom for the seadrome. Not only did it contain ammunition—bullets, bombs and small calibre shells—but case after case of seven-inch by three-inch cylinders of liquid Tetalyne, the most deadly explosive known to man.

For a moment he hardly dared breathe, for fear that movement of his lungs might set off some of the Tetalyne.

But, presently, he got a grip on himself, cursed softly and walked over to the nearest case. He knew that cold minimized the deadliness of Tetalyne by a good three-quarters. It was heat and detonation that set it off. That was why it was always stored in sub-zero temperature.

BENDING OVER the case, he stared down at the ends of one or two of the cylinders that stuck up above the sawdust and mohair. Absently he realized that this particular type was used in fifty pound aerial bombs—the type used on strafing pursuit ships.

The major portion of his brain, however, was thinking of other things. And a crazy, insane plan was taking form inside his head. Little by little his eyes narrowed, and his face became grim with savage reckless determination.

For just the fraction of a second he hesitated, then reached out with his left hand and pulled one of the cylinders from out of the case. Contact with its cold surface sent little ripples racing up and down his spine. He started to put it back, cursed and picked it up again.

Motionless, he let his eyes rove about the room once more. On the far side was a small door. It was more of a panel than a door. Its bottom edge was a good three feet from the floor. And there was a heavy clamp lock on the inside. A look at it and he realized that it was the opening to a loading chute that lead up toward the main deck.

Hugging the Tetalyne cylinder against his chest, so that it wouldn't possibly knock against anything, he walked over to the panel, stuffed his gun in his pocket a moment and undamped the lock. Standing to one side, just in case, he slowly pulled the panel back on its hinges and peered around the edge.

What he saw was a belt loading conveyor that slanted upward at a twenty-degree angle. The belt was motionless, and the hod-shaped platforms, fixed to it at even spacing, were empty.

The lower half was lighted up by the reflection of the storeroom bulb. But the top half, as he bent his head and looked up, was faintly bathed in the pale light of early dawn.

Dawn!

Hugging the Tetalyne cylinder closer he used his other hand to pull himself up onto the bottom part of the belt. And then, monkey style, but much slower, he went up the loading belt a step at a time. Salt air rushing down upon him cleared his brain and lent renewed strength to his tired muscles.

Two feet from the top outlet, he stopped, braced himself and inched upward until he could see over the lip. He found himself looking out over small platform toward the dawn-grayed swells of the Atlantic.

To the right of the platform, a flight of three steps lead up to the main deck. After rapidly reviewing the course he had been traveling since his escape, he judged himself to be somewhere near the southern end of the seadrome.

It took him but half a minute to slide out onto the small platform and find out. The result sent the blood surging through his veins like liquid fire.

He was ten feet from the eastern end of the northeast corner passenger building and looking straight at the Red Destroyer in its elevator platform cradle! Great streamers of milkish vapor were pouring out from its cone-shaped tail. The side section door was still down and—

His heart seemed to shrivel up inside of him as his eyes swept to the nose. The nose was bare!

Curly Brooks was gone!

CHAPTER 13
THE CRIMSON PATROL

CURLY BROOKS was gone! The words crashed through his brain like the booming of heavy cannon. In the same second he cursed himself bitterly for not coming back after his pal sooner.

But there was no time for bitter thought. Gun clamped in his right hand, Tetalyne cylinder clutched in his left, he sneaked up the three steps, slid across about ten feet of open deck and flattened himself against the rear wall of the passenger building.

And it was not until then that the sound of voices came to

him above the throbbing of the Red Destroyer's tuning-up gas rocket exhaust.

The voices were harsh and grating—Black voices! And although he was positive that they were speaking English he was unable to make out individual words. And then, suddenly—

"—did kill Ayres, I'll find you in hell someday, and even up double, so help me God!"

Curly's voice!

Dusty slid along the wall. The light toward the east was coming up fast The shadows of night were flitting away, and even small objects were beginning to take on clear shape and form. In the matter of minutes the deck bulbs that lighted up the seadrome would no longer be needed.

All that, Dusty realized and dismissed in an instant. The one thing that mattered now was Curly Brooks. Those devils had taken him down off the nose of the Red Destroyer and were grilling him. Hell, where was Agent 10? Hadn't he made any effort to contact either of them? He'd told the Intelligence man to try and meet them at the eastern end of the drome. Perhaps, Jack had been captured.

Dusty stopped guessing as he sidled tiger-like up to the corner of the building. Holding his breath he inched his head forward and peered around. The sight made things swim crazily for the second. Standing back to him was Curly Brooks, arms roped behind his back. Beside him, also back to, was a figure in the uniform of the Black Invaders. His arms were also pinned behind his back. One glance and Dusty knew. The second figure was Jack Horner!

In front of the pair stood Fire-Eyes, the Black Hawk, and a guard. The Black commander was talking, his voice booming out.

"You will die, Agent 10, in exactly five minutes! I give you five minutes so that you may fully realize what this last meeting means. It is my desire that you take into death with you, complete knowledge of the fate of your cursed country. For years you have been a small thorn in our sides. In Asia and in Europe you gave us much trouble. Had you performed such services for the Blacks, you would now be a man in high position. But you did not, and so you die. Nothing can save you. Your friend, Captain Ayres, is dead. His body floating somewhere out there!"

Fire-Eyes paused and swept his great long arm seaward. Blood-red filmed Dusty's eyes, but he had sense enough not to move. With Curly and Jack in the way, he could not possibly get at the others. For the moment it was a waiting game.

Then came Jack Horner's voice.

"Do what you like, and go to hell!"

A terrible roar bellowed from behind the green mask. The gauntleted fist smashed out. Jack Horner's body rose clear off the deck, turned in mid-air and came down with a sickening thud.

Dusty started to leap around the corner of the building, but instantly checked himself for two reasons. One, was memory of Jack Horner's words about the steel-mesh bullet-proof uniform worn by Fire-Eyes. And the second was the sight of a shouting Black soldier rushing down the runway. He was bellowing at the top of his voice, and waving his arms like a windmill. Dusty couldn't understand the words, for the man was shouting in his native tongue.

But he instantly guessed that it was something important. As the guard covered Curly, both Fire-Eyes and the Black Hawk spun around and raced toward him. They met him fifty yards away. And then began about fifteen seconds of wild arm waving and a conglomeration of thundering voices.

Suddenly Fire-Eyes grabbed hold of the Hawk, roared something at him and pointed back at the Red Destroyer. The Hawk nodded and spun around. In the same instant Fire-Eyes spun in the opposite direction and went bounding up the runway in great long giant strides, and lost himself to view as he turned a corner.

The Hawk raced toward the Red Destroyer, yelling at the guard covering Curly. And as he came close enough, Dusty snapped into lightning-like action.

He leaped around the corner, gun out.

"Down, Curly—down!"

It was perhaps a split second before Curly dropped flat, without even turning. But it was time enough for the guard to leap to one side and swing his gun.

THE PICTURE flashed before Dusty's eyes. The Hawk, not bothering to draw his gun, was swinging himself up onto the drop section of the Red Destroyer. And the Black guard was swinging his gun. A choice to be made in no time at all.

But Dusty had already made the choice. He had snapped his body sidewise, flung his gun hand across his chest and pulled the trigger.

The two shots blended into one sound.

A sledge hammer smashed against his left shoulder blade and knocked him forward. He bellowed out, twisted around on one foot and flung out his gun hand against the wall of the passenger building for support. He touched it in the nick of time. He was already falling, the Tetalyne cylinder still hugged against his chest.

Shouting, cursing in the same breath, he shoved himself back onto his heels and turned. Out the corner of his eye he caught a glimpse of three figures stretched out on the deck. One was Curly, and the other two wore Black uniforms.

And then his eyes leaped to the Red Destroyer. The drop section was swinging up into place. Something roared and Dusty's hand jumped. He saw a glistening groove suddenly appear on the underneath side of the closing drop section.

Dropping his gun, he transferred the Tetalyne cylinder to his right hand. His arm snapped back, snapped forward again. Something zipped through the closing plane door, as he fell on his face.

A split second later there was a terrific roar inside the Red Destroyer. Dusty felt the deck shake and tremble. Then a sound like the world ripping in two blasted out. And instantly following came an ear-piercing scream akin to a thousand dynamos running at full speed on dry bearings.

Louder and louder it grew in intensity until it seemed that both ocean and sky were giving off the horrible noise. The deck rocked and trembled. Then the Red Destroyer leaped forward.

Even as it moved it became no more than a crimson blurr that his eyes could not possibly follow.

A quarter of a mile of the U-shaped trough melted to the deck like so much tin in a blast furnace. Then the runway on the left side spouted smoke, sparks and flame. Two hangars folded up like matchwood. A passenger building fell apart in a smoky shower. And a repair depot vanished in thin air.

All in the matter of a split second.

Then something high in the air—no more than a shadow— pinwheeled about, end over end. It dropped, and the crest of a rolling swell miles away belched up a great shower of foam and spray.

"Done—done for!"

As Dusty shouted, be became aware that the seadrome was rocking with sound—the sound of explosions, airplane engines, and screaming lungs.

He lurched to his feet, and staggered over to Curly Brooks was muttering like a crazy man. Dusty grabbed the ropes that bound him with one hand, and slapped him hard across the face with the other.

"Shut up—hold still—we've got to move!"

Curly gasped and went limp as Dusty turned him over. It took him less than a minute to get his pal's arms free. Then he jerked him to his feet and shouted in his ear.

"Help me with Jack!"

Curly's eyes cleared and he nodded.

"Sure!"

Dusty didn't waste words. He bent down, scooped up the

dead Black's gun and then grabbed hold of Agent 10's feet. Curly grabbed the upper part.

"To the left—around the passenger building!" Dusty yelled, starting forward. "Don't stop for anything—I've got a gun!"

His body was burning with pain, but he didn't even notice it. Hugging Jack Horner's feet under his crooked left arm, gun ready in his right, he plunged around the corner of the passenger building to the ten-foot wide passage on the sea side.

Where there had been panic a few moments ago, the seadrome was now a place of utter chaos. Blacks were running pell-mell in all directions. Planes were taking off, with men clinging to the wings. And the drome itself was heaving in the rolling swells as explosion after explosion ripped and tore its underdecks apart.

For the first quarter of a mile Dusty could have had a thousand guns, and there would have been no need of them. The Blacks had gone completely haywire; it is doubtful if even one of them noticed the two figures that raced up the outside passage carrying a third figure between them.

BUT, AS they neared the ramp leading down to where their hidden plane was moored, three wild-eyed Blacks came charging blindly around the corner of a building and plowed right into them.

As Dusty went spinning over backward he heard his gun roar; heard, too, the agonizing scream that followed an instant later. The next thing he realized, he was the center of a writhing heap of thrashing arms and legs.

The gun had been knocked from his hand when he hit the

deck. But he still had his fists, and he used them as he had never used them before.

Bellowing encouragement to Curly, he lashed out in all directions, thrilling to the core as he felt his knuckles crash against jawbone. But he was by no means escaping other fists. They slammed and pounded against him until it seemed that every drop of strength had been sapped from his body. He was but a dead man carrying on from the momentum of life.

And then, suddenly, hands gripped his arms and a voice roared in his ears.

"Hey! They're cold! Snap it up! There's more coming!"

He gaped up into Curly's blood-shot eyes. One Black was gone. Another hung head down over the guard rail. And the third was a crumpled hulk on the deck, half sprawled across the helpless Agent 10, who lay gaping stupidly at the dawn-lighted sky. And off to the left, a group of Blacks were pounding across the runway toward them.

"Take Jack down, Curly!" Dusty barked, his brain clearing in a flash. "Untie him—take him aboard. Yell when set—I'll hold off these rats!"

He finished by giving Curly a shove, scooped up a rifle that one of the Blacks had dropped, and bracing himself against the wall of the building, smashed two quick shots into the advancing Blacks. Two of them went flat and the others skidded to a halt and ducked behind the front corner of the building.

Shrinking back, Dusty shot a side glance toward the ramp. Curly was halfway down it, Agent 10 slung over his shoulder. He waited until Curly disappeared in the murky shadows below, then slapped a single shot along the side of the building and sprinted across the open space to the lip of the ramp.

As he reached it something twanged off the metal deck a foot away. A second something whined past his ear, so close that his ear seemed to actually sting. And then he was tumbling down into the shelter of the ramp.

Checking his tumble he crawled back toward the lip, flattened himself on his stomach and stuck an eye around the corner. Two of the Blacks were stealing toward him. A snap shot from his rifle got one, and the other melted out of sight.

He started to let go a warning shot, when suddenly he noticed the cartridge clip. It was empty. The bullet in the firing chamber was the only one he had left.

He cursed and lay straining his ears for Curly's signal. The seconds ticking by seemed like years. He glanced longingly at another rifle on the deck about thirty feet away, tore his eyes off it and cursed. He'd be drilled before he got halfway to it. Damn, Curly, why in hell was he taking so long? At most any second the damn Blacks might suspect, and rush him.

He risked a quick look around the corner and groaned. His fear was coming true. Four Blacks were running toward the ramp!

"Dusty!"

Never had a voice sounded so welcome as did Curly's ringing up from below. He shoved the rifle out, drew a quick bead on the nearest Black and pulled the trigger. He got a flash look of a black uniformed figure spinning over backward. But that was all. Feet hardly touching the ramp, he raced down it, swerved left at the bottom and forward to the landing steps.

A wild shout of joy burst from his lips as he caught sight of the amphibian. Curly Brooks had his blood-caked face sticking up out of the cabin ceiling trap-door was waving at him crazily. The plane had been cast free, and the swells were taking it away from the steps.

Down them Dusty went in one step and flung himself flat on the smooth wing. The instant he touched, his arms and legs were working crab-like and shoving his body toward the center section.

Three feet from it, Curly heaved himself up and out, grabbed his outstretched hand and pulled him head first down into the cabin.

The next thing that Dusty's whirling head became conscious of was that he was kicking the electric starter and ruddering the plane out from under the over-hanging lips of the seadrome.

Faintly he heard the crackle of guns behind him, heard fingers of steel smack into the cabin ceiling of the plane. But all that was but secondary reaction. The ship was quivering beneath him, and the engine, mounted topside, was blasting out its song of power. Swells rushed toward him, splashed salt drops against the forward windows. And then as the hull went up on its step, and the plane cleared, swirling air wiped the windows dry.

THROTTLE WIDE open, and Dep wheel well back, Dusty sent the amphibian roaring up into the dawn sky. And so intent was he upon putting distance between the plane and the drome that it wasn't for several minutes that he suddenly realized with a start that the sky to the south was speckled with darting and zooming planes. And that the southern horizon was black with heavy smoke.

Leveling off automatically, he gaped popeyed in that direction.

"My God! What the hell?"

As he roared out the words, he slammed the plane over on wing and went tearing around to the south. He could see the planes clearly. Some of them were Black ships—but the majority of them were American. He let go the controls, half turned his head and pointed.

"Look fellows!" he shouted. "Yank planes!"

He started to say more, but the grin on Agent 10's white face checked him. He scowled questioningly at the Intelligence man.

"Guess they didn't have to come after all," said Agent 10 quietly.

Dusty's head hurt too much to figure that one out. He cursed and leaned back.

"Now what the hell do you mean?" he snapped.

"When we split," replied the other, "I struck the radio room by chance. The operator was half asleep. Put him all the way, and then contacted our Atlantic fleet and asked for help. I—"

"But the defense of the seadrome?" Dusty broke it. "You said—"

"Sure," the other, cut him off. "But, there was a chance of a surprise attack. I could see you from the radio shack. Saw you both, with Fire-Eyes and the Hawk by that thing. It looked like curtains for you, so the only thing I could do was try and get an S.O.S. through. At least other Black stations that picked it up couldn't, warn the drome because I was in the radio room. To make sure that nothing would come in, I busted a few things before I left."

"Well, I'll be—!" grunted Dusty.

"And that's not all he did, kid!" spoke up Curly. "He sneaked down, and pulled me off that damn thing. The others had gone after you. But, they nailed us again. And then you popped up again. Hell, I've been a drag anchor to this party. I...."

"Hey, look!" burst out Jack Horner. "A couple of Yanks tearing in on us. My God, they think we're Blacks!"

In a flash Dusty spun back toward the front, saw the two bullet-spitting U.S. Navy planes thundering down, and grabbed for the radio.

"Navy—don't!" he bellowed into the transmitter tube. "We're Yanks escaping!"

Instantly the planes ceased firing. But they continued to swoop down until they were abreast of the amphibian. Across the air space Dusty saw two pairs of steely eyes clamped upon him. He let go of the Dep wheel, half rose out of his seat and ripped off the Black tunic that he wore. The nearest Yank pilot swung in almost to the wingtip, took another good look, then grinned and waved his hand.

An instant later Dusty saw him lean toward his transmitter tube; heard the crackling words coming out of the speaker unit.

"O.K., Captain Ayres! Go home and wash your face. It needs it. Everything is O.K. We've got these lads on the run, and the Old Man is giving their battle wagons hell farther south. S'long!"

Dusty settled back in the seat, turned and glanced back at the seadrome. Heavy navy shells were tearing into it. Already the western end was under water. About its twisted and torn deck figures were still racing about. He stared at them a minute. "Hope the hell one of them is Fire-Eyes!" he grated.

"Don't hope too much," came Agent 10's voice. "I'll bet a year's pay that he was the first to leave it. Curly told me that he beat it forward, just after he'd knocked me cold. He was probably on his way then."

"I wonder what the hell that was all about?" muttered Dusty. "The Hawk tried to take off in the Red Destroyer."

"I can make a good guess, now that I think back," said Jack Horner. "One thing I forgot to bust in the radioroom was the outgoing message recorder. If you ask me, the operator came out of his slumber, saw what had been sent out—and warned Fire-Eyes. Probably the Hawk intended to rip up our Atlantic fleet."

Dusty nodded, and his eyes went agate.

"Yeah!" he grated. "Probably! But it was his last act, damn his hide. At least he's sunk—and sunk for good!"

And then at the very next moment, as though Fate itself had timed it exactly, the signal light blinked and a voice spoke out of the cabin unit.

"Calling Captain Ayres—Calling Captain Ayres on seven-nine-six!"

Dusty spun the wave-length dial to seven-nine-six.

"On contact. Go ahead!"

"My congratulations, captain. I understand that you won again. Make the most of it, for it will be your last victory!"

"My God!" cried Curly, as the set clicked silent. "He couldn't have lived! I tell you, that thing went to the bottom. And besides—the explosion!"

Dusty said nothing. His eyes met Jack Horner's. The Intelligence man shrugged.

"I wondered," Horner said. "Didn't get a close look at him. Oh, well, that's another of his pinch hitters out of the way. We'll get him, yet!"

"The very next time!" growled Dusty. "The very next time, so help me, God! And—and a couple of his damn brood right now!"

"Hey, Dusty, nix!" Curly shouted. "Let the other lads have some fun. My God, haven't you had enough exercise for a while? And besides, I'm hungry as hell, man!"

"And me too!" Jack Horner chimed in.

Dusty relaxed. He was suddenly very, very tired. Every inch of his body ached unbearably. Added to that, he was twice as hungry, too.

"That is an idea, isn't it?" he muttered thickly. "Yeah, I guess the rats can wait until after we eat!"

And with that, he banked the amphibian around and headed it southwest toward native shores.

POPULAR PUBLICATIONS
HERO PULPS

LOOK FOR MORE SOON!

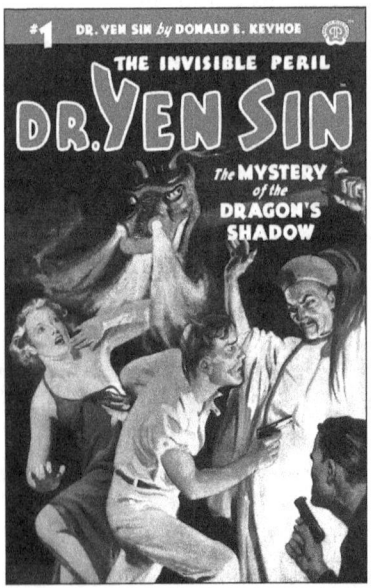

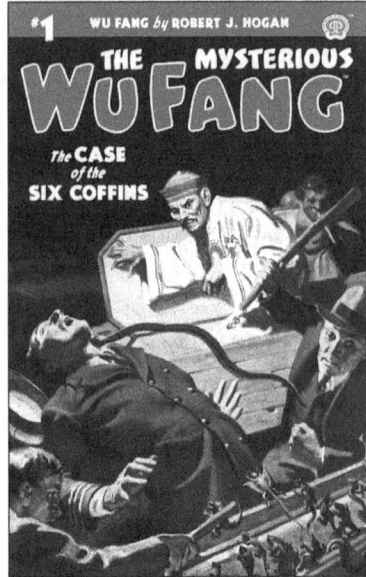